Howl

A Small and Heavy Adventure

Miles Salter

First published in Great Britain in 2015
by Caboodle Books Ltd
Copyright © Miles Salter 2015

A Catalogue record for this book is available
from the British Library.

ISBN 978 0 9933000 1 1

Cover by Richard McDougall
Illustrations by Martin Cottam
Page Layout by Highlight Type Bureau Ltd
Printed by CPI Group (UK) Ltd, Croydon, CR0 4YY

The paper and board used in the paperback by
Caboodle Books Ltd are natural recyclable products
made from wood grown in sustainable forests.
The manufacturing processes conform to the environmental
regulations of the country of origin.

Caboodle Books Ltd
Riversdale, 8 Rivock Avenue, Steeton, BD20 6SA
www.authorsabroad.com

Dedicated to the memory of Trevor Brooker,
1949 – 2014.

About The Author

Miles Salter is a writer, musician and storyteller based in York. He writes fiction, poetry and journalism. His previous books include 'A Song For Nicky Moon', shortlisted for *The Times / Chicken House* children's writing award, and two books of poetry, 'The Border' and 'Animals'. 'Howl' is his first book for younger children. His journalism has appeared in newspapers including *The Sunday Times*, *Daily Telegraph*, *The Independent* and *The Guardian*.

Miles is also Director of York Literature Festival and is a visiting lecturer in creative writing at Leeds Trinity University. He lives in York with his family, two cats, eight guitars and a pile of books he hasn't read yet.

Miles often visits schools to give workshops and performances. Find out more at www.miles-salter.co.uk or via Trevor Wilson at Authors Abroad:

Authors Abroad and Caboodle Books Ltd
Riversdale
8 Rivock Avenue
Steeton
BD20 6SA
United Kingdom
Phone: (01535) 656015

Email: trevor@caboodlebooks.co.uk

Acknowledgments

'Howl' began as a flash in my head one day in 2009. It took six years to write, changing many times along the way. Scenes were written, then deleted, characters changed, and plot lines amended. After years of work, drafts and false starts, the old adage about perspiration and inspiration rings very true.

I'm indebted to Laura West at David Higham Associates for the many hours she spent advising on the manuscript, and for her enthusiasm and patience. Thanks Laura.

Thanks to Trevor Wilson and the team at Caboodle Books and Authors Abroad, and to everybody at Macmillan Marketing Services.

Thanks to Alison Morgan, Lizzi Linklater and Pauline Kirk who commented on early drafts, and to Daniel Egan and Robin Morgan who said they liked it, long before it was finished.

Finally, thanks to everybody who reads the book. A story only lives in the mind of the reader – so thank you for bringing it to life. Do write to me and let me know what you think. I'd love to hear from you. And let me know if you'd like me to visit your school.

Miles Salter
York
November 2015

Part One:
Bad News

Chapter One

'James Small, stand up!'

Miss Lipps' voice boomed through the hall. Our head teacher was looking straight at me.

I got to my feet. The pupils of Rigor Mourtice Community Primary were looking up at me, James Small, football fan, skate boarding demon, lover of marshmallows, member of Year 5.

'What were you doing?' bellowed Miss Lipps. You didn't want to mess with Miss Lipps. Our headteacher was a great big barrel of a woman, tall and wide and loud and fierce. She'd been known to make kids cry just by saying their name. Loudly. Nothing Miss Lipps did was quiet.

'Nothing, Miss,' I said, in my best 'I am totally innocent of any crime' voice.

'Try again,' said Miss Lipps. She wasn't backing down.

'Erm...well...I was just saying to Neville,' I said, nodding at my best friend, 'that there seems to be a spider in Lucy Black's hair.'

Lucy Black was the biggest teacher's pet *ever*. She was so clever that she made Einstein look like a dumbo. Lucy had dark hair and a small mean mouth and she never, ever smiled. She was an expert in speed tongue poking. She could turn around, poke her tongue at me, and turn back again in 0.3 seconds. She'd had a lot of practice. We were *not* best mates.

'A spider?' asked Miss Lipps, in that *really* annoying way

that adults have of repeating what you said a few seconds before.

I nodded, and watched Lucy put her hand up slowly to her hair. The spider clambered onto her knuckles and when Lucy lowered her hand, she saw it and screamed. The spider, who obviously wasn't used to being screamed at, fell onto her shiny black shoes, his furry legs moving fast as he scuttled across the floor. Hysteria began to spread as the girls moved away from the scuttling creature, saying stuff like 'gross' and 'yuk' and 'this is the worst thing that has happened to me, ever, I think I might die in the next thirty two seconds'. Mr Marsh picked up the spider and escorted it from the hall.

'Tell me James,' shouted Miss Lipps, 'did the spider get there by itself?'

'Erm...think it parachuted in,' I said quietly. Neville giggled into his hand.

Miss Lipps glared at me.

'Did you put it there?' she said.

'I might have given it some help, Miss,' I said in a small voice. Some of the children sniggered. The spider had fallen onto my head, just as we'd all started singing 'All Things Bright and Beautiful'. I scooped it up, showed Neville, and carefully held it over Lucy Black's head.

'And why were you talking?'

'We were discussing the whole spider situation, Miss. And before that, I was telling Neville about this massive green bogey I found in my nose this morning and...'

'Enough!' bellowed Miss Lipps, rolling her eyes. 'You should be setting an example, James Small! Now can we please finish the last verse?'

We sang the last verse of *All Things Bright and Beautiful*. I tried to look like I was singing it properly, but I wasn't very good at being very good, especially if it involved sitting still, behaving and not talking. I liked talking to Neville about really important stuff, like football, Playstation, or how far a speeding fart can travel in three seconds flat.

The song finished, which was a relief. Miss Lipps started up again.

'Now children, as some of you will know, Mr Watts is recovering from his knee operation and won't be in for the rest of the term, and I'd like to introduce our new teacher.'

Her eyes swivelled to the side.

A strange looking man was standing at the edge of the hall. He was tall and thin, with arms that were too long for the long green coat he wore. Brown hair streamed back from the top of his head and tumbled past his collar. His eyes sat in deep and hollow sockets. Above them sprawled two bushy black eyebrows that almost touched above his long nose. Angular sideburns stretched over his sunken cheeks, like arrows pointing to the ground. He didn't look like a man who laughed much. He'd probably get on very well with Lucy.

I wasn't crazy about Mr Watts, who smelt funny and was always on about the battle of Hastings and had a habit of making us draw maps of Noirshire. He also had a lot to say about Magna Carta, which was a very early form of ice cream. But it took me about half a quarter of a microsecond to realise that Mr Watts was better than the new man.

'Children, please give Mr Grindell a round of applause.'

I wanted to say, 'But Miss, he hasn't done anything yet,' but decided I'd better keep quiet.

As the hall filled with clapping, Neville dug me in the ribs.

'He looks like a proper weirdo,' Neville said. I laughed, and tried to cover my mouth, but the sound still leaked out. Miss Lipps gave Neville and me one of her hard stares, then turned back to the new teacher.

'I do apologise, Mr Grindell,' said Miss Lipps. 'Most of our children are very good, but we do have one or two who can be a little bit...challenging.'

I sighed. It wasn't a big school and Neville and me were *always* being noticed, even though the stuff we did wasn't that bad. Mostly, we were just having fun. But 'fun' and 'being good' didn't always go together. Like the time in Year 2 when we let the class stick insects, Michael and Jackson, out of their box, and let them loose in the girls' changing room. (You should have heard the screaming! It was like a horror movie. With stick insects. And without any blood.) Or the time in Year 4 when I dared Neville to eat a daffodil, and he actually did, and twenty minutes later he was sick over Lucy Black's maths book. Little bits of daffodil splattered over her sums. She was *really* cross. It was long multiplication, and she'd got all the sums right. 'The page is ruined!' she'd complained. I pointed out that the daffodil added colour to the page, but I still got into trouble.

Now we were in Year 5 and we had to be sensible. We had to set an example, which meant no fun at all. We couldn't run in the corridor. And we were not allowed to make any of the Year 2s eat worms or tell them that the Headteacher wanted to see them straight away, or that their Grandma had gone to hospital because her nose had swollen to an unbelievably massive size and was actually sending out signals to Aliens from the planet Bot.

Oh no. Year 5 was a lot less fun.

Miss Lipps turned to Mr Grindell.

'Would you like to say a few words?' Miss Lipps said.

'Thank you, Miss Lipps,' said the man. He coughed as he stood up. He was very tall, and he bounced a little as he walked to the front of the hall. Neville's mouth gaped open as he stared at this strange new teacher.

'Eurgh,' said Neville.

'What?' I hissed.

'His hands.'

I looked. The new teacher's hands were covered in thick, dark hair.

'Yuk,' I said.

Mr Grindell stared at the rows of children.

'Well,' said Mr Grindell. 'Greetings, children.' He didn't sound enthusiastic. His voice was a low rumble and his tongue flicked between his teeth like a thin snake.

Some of the girls moved back, horrified. Lucy Black and Katie Nicholls stared, their mouths open wide.

'I'm looking forward,' said Mr Grindell, 'to spending time getting to know you all. I'm going to be 5D's new form teacher. I will also be in charge of science at the school, and I am delighted to be here.' But he didn't look delighted, not at all. He looked like a man who'd just spent the last five years thinking about slowly drowning in a cold and smelly swamp.

Neville and I looked at each other in horror. 5D was our class! Mr Grindell was going to be our teacher!

'The other exciting thing,' said Miss Lipps, 'is we'll be having our annual school concert on the evening of October 31st. We'll be practising hard with your singing and your lovely recorders.'

I nudged Neville.

'Lovely recorders?' I said. 'Whenever my sister plays hers I want to immediately die. I mean, have you heard a recorder when it's played not very well? It's total musical agony.'

My sister, Emma, was in Year 4. I tried to avoid her whenever possible. But this could be hard sometimes, as we lived in the same house.

'Right,' said Miss Lipps. 'Have a good rest of term,

everybody. I'm sure it's going to be absolutely wonderful.' She pressed a button on the old stereo at the front of the hall. Panpipes played as we filed out. I looked over my shoulder and caught sight of Mr Grindell's dark eyes following me as I walked into the corridor. Then he wandered over to have a word with Miss Lipps.

We walked to our classroom as quickly as we could.

'Go on,' Neville said, nudging me with his elbow. 'Draw a picture of Mr Grindell. I dare you.'

I hesitated. I was good at cartoons, but didn't want to get caught. But Neville kept saying 'Go on James, go on James,' and joined in. Looking nervously at the door, I reached for the white board marker and drew a cartoon of Mr Grindell, with long arms and flicking tongue. I gave him hands like claws, and a wild and crazy look in his eyes.

I put the pen down and Neville picked it up and wrote the words 'Very Very Weird' in large letters and an arrow pointing to Mr Grindell's head. By this time everybody was laughing, apart from Lucy Black who sat there with her arms folded, scowling at me with eyes that said 'you'll never get away with this, loser.'

Meanwhile, the room boomed with laughter. A couple of the kids were pointing at the board, rocking backwards and forwards on their chairs. This got me going even more, so I started to pretend I was Mr Grindell, and walked up and down with a floppy walk and bulging eyes.

'Greetings, children,' I said, with my deepest voice. I flicked my tongue out. The whole class was in stitches, hooting and banging the tables.

And then the door at the end of the corridor swung open. Everybody scrambled for their seats. I ran to mine and managed to get in it just before a shadow appeared in the doorway.

Mr Grindell's face was long and tight when he looked in the

classroom. It took about 0.0000000003 seconds for the children in 5D to be sat at their desks, quiet and straight, with serious faces that said 'we would never ever ever do anything naughty. We are the best-behaved children in the whole of Noirshire. When we are at home we do the gardening and enjoy doing Maths problems and we never watch television or eat sweets.'

Mr Grindell walked slowly into the room, scowling at the class. He took off his green coat and hung it on the back of the door, then put his hands together and made his knuckles crack before waving his long fingers. Then he turned to the board. I gulped. He had seen my drawing.

'Who,' said Mr Grindell, his eyes narrowing as he looked down on the class, 'did this?' His voice was a thin hiss.

Silence. Nobody moved. Grindell's beady eyes roamed around the room, looking at our faces.

After a moment, Lucy Black put her hand up in the air.

'Mr Grindell,' she said. 'It was Neville Heavy and James Small.'

'Small and Heavy, come here,' said Mr Grindell. Neville and I looked at each other. I could see Neville swallow as we walked to the front of the class. Mr Grindell loomed above us, his eyes scanning our faces. He had yellow teeth and breath that smelt like dog food and sewers, only not as pleasant.

'So,' he said, 'it's true about you two being naughty. I will deal with you later. Now go and sit down.'

Neville looked at me, rolling his eyes. I knew *exactly* what he was thinking.

Small and Heavy were in trouble.

Again.

Chapter Two

'I want you to write out a hundred times, 'I won't be naughty in Mr Grindell's class again. Ever.' Our new teacher seemed to be enjoying himself as he slapped two sheets of paper in front of us.

It was the end of a long school day. Neville and I had to stay behind, watching sadly as everybody else in our class went out the door. Earlier, Mr Grindell had told everybody about the new classroom rules: No talking. No spitting. No burping. No vomiting in the bin.

We'd grinded our way through fractions, drawn a map of Ancient Rome (mine included Ye Olde Ancient Sweetshop and Ye Olde Playstation) and listened as Grindell lectured us on the properties of sulphur. He seemed to be interested in chemistry. I was itching to go. But now I had to write out lines.

Neville started first. I fidgeted. I got a rubber, then a pencil sharpener, then sharpened my pencil, then yawned, then I sharpened my pencil again. Then my pencil snapped, so I sharpened it again. Then I yawned, blew my nose and tied my shoelaces. Then my ear needed scratching. After about four minutes of fidgeting and sharpening and yawning and scratching, I started to write.

'I won't be naughty in Mr Grindell's class again,' I wrote. 'Ever.'

The first time I wrote it out, I was a little bit bored. The fourth time I was very bored. By the time I got to line twenty I was so unbelievably bored that I suspected I might have very bored disease. It would happen like this:

Me: Mum! Look! I've got bored disease. My skin's covered in terrible green boils. I feel dizzy. I don't think I can stand up much longer. Look! I'm actually wobbling! Help!

Mum: Oh my poor bored child, the terrible boredom disease has got you! Quick! In the car! We must get you to hospital at once!

(At the hospital...)
Doctor: Why is this child wobbling?
Mum: I think he's dying, Doctor.
Doctor: Dying? What of?
Mum: Boredom, doctor.
Doctor: Good gracious, we didn't think it was physically possible! Quick, nurse, get the video camera! This evidence could be vitally important in preventing other children from dying of boredom.

Mum: But Doctor, is it serious?
Doctor: We must operate very soon or he will very much be dead.
Mum: But James hasn't had his tea!
Doctor: What has caused your boredom infection, James?
Me: I have an evil teacher who made me write lines.
Doctor: Your teacher must be reprimanded straight away. Look at the damage he has done! We can't have teachers behaving like that!
Mum: What about James's tea?
Doctor: Nurse, get this boy some tea. And be sure to include marshmallows!

I sighed, wrote some more lines and eventually got to line

77. It was hard to read my writing, because I was racing so much to get to the end of the line.

'Hurry up,' said Grindell, irritated. 'I haven't got all night.' He looked out of the window.

Neville had almost finished, his page full of neat, tidy writing. Neville was always better at school stuff than me. He was cleverer, and we both knew it. He read more books and knew more stuff. Neville's dad was a vicar, and was known around town as Rev'd Heavy.

Neville's family lived in the vicarage, a big old house with high ceilings. It was right next to St Cuthbert's Church, where Rev'd Heavy was in charge. Neville had to help by ringing the Church bells every Sunday with an old woman called Janet and a tall man called Dennis. Neville wasn't crazy about bell ringing. He said it gave him a headache, which wasn't surprising. Big Bill, the famous bell in the church, was well known in the town. This was because it was out of tune, and sounded like a bell that just couldn't be bothered.

Neville's bedroom was really big (about three times bigger than mine) and it was where he kept his collection of dinosaur fossils and encyclopaedias and his electronics gear. He was always messing about with remote control cars and bits of computers, or doing bits of metalwork. If you needed to get something fixed, you asked Neville. He was a genius at mechanics and electronics. By the time he was six he was taking computers to pieces and putting them back together. Some of the kids called him 'Nerdy Neville' – and it was true he wore spectacles, but he was still my best mate. And I was proud that he was so clever.

When I was in Year Two, for my birthday, I was given a remote control car (a phantom XL9 in fireball red, which everybody knows is the fastest colour available). But my stupid sister, who was little and annoying, stamped on it. Afterwards, the car made a strange whirring sound and wouldn't go. When Neville heard about what happened, he said, 'I'll have a look at it.' I took the Phantom to his house and he bent over it with a screwdriver. I watched as Neville made little humming noises as he tweaked the parts, and twenty minutes later the car was working fine. We were best mates after that.

He liked coming to my house because we had biscuits or cake, which he wasn't allowed at home. EVER. Neville's family were strict. Every day, Neville had to tidy his room, do bell ringing and practice his reading, writing or Maths. That was why he was naughty with me. He just needed to let off a bit of steam, as my Dad would say.

If there was one thing Neville loved more than anything, it was cake. If he came round and Mum had some lemon drizzle, or carrot cake, Neville's eyes would widen in delight. He would peek into the kitchen, his eyes lighting up when he saw flapjack or Victoria sponge, and he'd wolf down the cake in about 3.4 seconds. He could have had a new world record for fastest cake wolfing. There'd be a crumb of lemon drizzle on Neville's lip. But that was it. It was impressive.

I watched as Neville took his work up to Mr Grindell, who sneered at it, scrunched the paper into a little ball, and tossed it into the bin. Neville stared in disbelief.

'Don't do it again,' boy, sneered Grindell, his eyeballs about four inches from Neville's.

Neville twitched. 'N-no Sir,' he said, in a small voice.

'Now get out of here!' Grindell yelled, pointing to the door.

'Bye James,' Neville said softly on his way out. I heard the outside door close and Neville's feet on the concrete. I sighed, counted my lines. I had thirty-two to go.

Grindell kept looking out of the window. He was transfixed

by the moon that hung above the town. He made a strange noise – a mixture between a cough, a sigh, and a moan.

'Are you alright, Sir?' I asked, quietly.

Grindell looked at me with strange eyes, as if he wasn't really seeing me. When he spoke his voice was quiet and distant.

'You may depart,' he said, waving his hand.

He didn't have to tell me again. I grabbed my stuff, ran from the classroom, and left.

Outside, the wind whistled in the trees. I looked back and saw Grindell standing in the classroom, his body silhouetted, staring at the moon. He was motionless.

I shivered, then ran from the school, as fast as I could.

Chapter Three

At home, Mum wanted to talk to me.

'James,' she said. 'We need to have a little chat.'

Uh oh, I thought. A 'little chat' is *never* what it says it is. Whenever a 'little chat' happens, I always have to sit in Dad's study downstairs, and Mum comes in and tells me what I've done wrong and then I have to *go to my room and think about it*.

I shot a glance at Emma, who was sitting at the kitchen table, doing some sort of gel art for girls, the sort that involves puppies or fairies but never aliens or laser guns. Had she told Mum about what happened in assembly?

Emma had to be the biggest idiot sister in the known Universe. If I travelled to the other end of the Galaxy, I'd never find a more stupid, annoying, irritating sister. Unless, of course, there was a massive space station outside the planet that held a sign that said, in enormous neon letters: 'WARNING! Home of Universe's most stupid, annoying, irritating sister. Do not approach without anti-annoyance headgear and anti-irritation suit.'

I went to Dad's study. I sat in his chair, the big black leather one, like the chair in *Mastermind.* My feet dangled off the end. On the wall were Dad's certificates from his engineering work.

Mum came in, closed the door and sat down. I swallowed, and got ready for a lecture.

'Did you have to stay behind?' Mum asked. I nodded sadly,

then told her about our strange new teacher.

'I'm sure Mr Grindell is very nice,' said Mum, failing to listen to what I'd just said. Why do grown ups never get it? They're in their own world! Mum took four minutes to tell me to be good. I nodded and said 'Yes, Mum' about twelve times. When I thought our little chat was over, I realised she had something else to say.

'Dad's got some special work. In France,' said Mum.

I nodded. Dad often worked abroad. He helped people to design and build tunnels. A long time ago, before he met Mum, he worked on the Channel Tunnel, which is this massive big huge tunnel that goes from England to Zimbabwe.

'We've talked about it, and I'm going to go with him,' said Mum. 'We're leaving in a couple of days and we thought...'

'Okay,' I said. 'I'll go and live alone in the woods in a tent with only an airgun, a chainsaw and a huge packet of marshmallows?'

'Nice try, James,' smiled Mum. 'But that won't be happening. Actually, we thought you could stay with somebody. Just for a little while.'

'How long are you going for?' I asked.

'Two weeks,' Mum said.

'Two weeks! That's ages!'

'You'll be fine, sweetheart,' Mum said, kissing me on the head.

'Can I stay at Neville's?' I asked.

Mum frowned.

'Sorry, dear. We wanted to ask Neville's mum but with the new baby and everything...' Neville's mum had recently had a baby girl. Neville's sister was bald and had lines under her eyes and little pink lips and tiny fingers. When I asked Neville what he thought about the baby, all he said was, 'Lindsey cries. And stinks.'

'I'm staying with Nadia,' said Emma, poking her nose through the door. Nadia was Emma's best friend at school. Emma stuck a tongue out at me, as if to say 'I get to stay with a friend, but you don't! Nah!'

'So...who am I staying with?' I asked.

Mum smiled a wobbly-looking smile.

'We've found a lovely lady for you to stay with. An experienced child minder.'

'What?' I said. 'You're sending me to live with a complete stranger?'

Mum smiled. 'It's only for a short while, dear,' she said. 'You'll be fine with Mrs Winters.'

'Mrs Winters?'

Mum produced a piece of paper from her pocket and passed it to me. *The Mourtice Courier* was well known for its headlines like 'Mattress left on street' and 'Woman cuts finger on paper'. But Miss Lipps loved it whenever Rigor Mourtice Community Primary got in the paper.

I looked at the piece of paper in my hand.

'Child-minder available for long and short term assignments,' it said, and underneath was a picture of a grinning lady. 'New to the area.' She had small round spectacles and a couple of teeth missing. It took me about one microsecond to decide I didn't like the idea of sharing a house with this person.

'What a weirdo,' I said.

'Don't be unkind,' said Mum.

'What's she like?' I asked, suspiciously.

'You'll find out tomorrow,' said Mum. 'Dad is taking you around to see her after school.'

My heart sank. I was going to have to live with a strange old woman. She might be deaf. She might smell funny. She wouldn't know anything about football. I'd probably eat carrots and broccoli for two weeks and then I would actually starve! I went in the lounge. At the table, Emma was doing her homework. I turned the TV on. I let out a loud sigh.

'Something wrong?' Emma asked, smiling.

I poked my tongue at Emma. Then I realised, there was one good thing about Mum and Dad going away. At least I wouldn't have to live with my stupid sister for a while.

Chapter Four

Dad peered through the window at Number 1 Back Lane, then checked the address on his piece of paper.

'This is it,' said Dad, turning off the engine. He looked at me.

'What's up? You look worried.'

I stared out of the car window. From here, I could see across Rigor Mourtice. We were on the hill at the southern end of the town. Half a mile beneath us, the town lay in its valley, between hillsides. Our little town was a jumble of rooftops. To the North, and two hundred feet up a hill, lay the reservoir, its expanse of water glinting in the October sunshine.

I bit my lip. Dad was right. I *was* worried. I was about to meet a total stranger, and Mum and Dad expected me to live with them!

'I just have one question,' I said.

'Hmm?' asked Dad.

'What if she's a loony?'

'You'll be fine,' said Dad, in that half-jokey voice that grown ups use when they dismiss the concerns of children. I sighed loudly, in a way that showed I was NOT HAPPY with this whole situation. I also folded my arms, because that's what you need to do at times like this, to show you really mean business and should not be messed with.

'Come on James,' said Dad. 'Sulking doesn't suit you.'

We got out of the car and walked to the house. The front

door was a dark grey colour. There was a small brass plate that said 'Mrs Audrey Winters, W.I.C.U.' The cracks on the window panes reminded me of spider's webs. Dad knocked on the door. A short while later the door swung back with a low creak.

Before us was a tiny old woman. She could not have been more than five feet tall. Curly white hair sprang from her head like smoke from an explosion. Deep lines covered her face, and she had a long nose that held a pair of small round spectacles. Her eyes were bright, and above them were bushy eyebrows that seemed to have a life of their own. Grey and white hairs jutted out at various angles.

Beneath her ears were two silver earrings, shaped like the moon. She wore a red dress, with a dark green shawl spread across her shoulders. It was fastened together with a silver metal brooch. Her fingernails were an inch long. I noticed with a shudder that one of her fingers was missing. It was hard not to stare at this extraordinary person.

'Yes?' she said, frowning.

'Hello,' said Dad. 'We're looking for Mrs Winters.'

'Oh...ah...um...that is me,' said the little woman.

'My name is Dave Small. This is my son, James,' said Dad.

Mrs Winters looked at me.

'Very pleased to meet you,' she said, smiling. She extended some bony fingers to shake my hand. Only it wasn't much of a smile, because her mouth had several teeth missing.

'Come in,' she said.

We walked into a dark room. It was full of packing boxes, some with their lids opened. Pots and pans were strewn across the floor. Shelves were stacked with ancient books, some piled on top of each other, others with split spines and faded, dark red covers.

I peered at one book. I thought it said 'A Multitude Of Uses

For Poison' in faded gold writing, but when Mrs Winters saw I was looking at the book, she quickly removed it before I could be certain of the title. In a corner, sitting on a pile of boxes, was a ginger cat. His green eyes watched us warily as we came in.

'Excuse the mess,' she said. 'As you can see, things are still a little chaotic. I've only been here since last Wednesday. I haven't finished unpacking yet.'

The cat meowed loudly.

'Yes, yes, Clarence. Keep your fur on.' She looked at me. 'It takes him a while to get used to strangers, but he'll be fine soon enough.'

'What's that smell?' asked Dad. 'It's amazing.'

'I'm rather partial to cooking,' said Mrs Winters, looking at me. 'Would you like some cake?' Before I could reply, she went into the kitchen and opened the oven door. An aroma of chocolate cake filled the room as she pulled out a dark sponge, then proceeded to smother it with chocolate from a jug. A minute later, a table held three small plates and a massive cake. The smell filled my nose and my mouth began to water.

Seeing the interest in my face, she picked up a knife and cut a large piece of chocolate cake and placed it on a blue plate. She handed me a spoon.

'Delicious,' I said, as I ate three mouthfuls in ten seconds.

'I suppose I will need to fill in a form?' asked Dad. 'In case of any accidents?'

'Ah. Yes,' said Mrs Winters. 'I have one here.'

She produced a piece of paper. 'Audrey Winters, Childminder,' it said at the top. Underneath were four addresses, each one crossed out. The addresses were written on top of each other.

'You've moved around a bit,' said Dad. He took out a pen and began to fill in his details.

'Yes,' said the lady. 'My work keeps me on the move.'

'I see you have letters after your name,' said Dad. 'W.I.C.U. I haven't seen that combination before. What does it stand for?'

Mrs Winters' smile fell for a moment. She looked at the floor. 'Oh, erm, well...' She paused briefly, fluttering her eyelids, then recovered. 'It is a long time since I studied. Do you know, I've forgotten what the letters are for. But let's not worry about that now.'

'Right,' said Dad. He peered out of the window.

'What an unusual garden,' he said. 'You have some amazing looking plants.'

'Oh yes,' said Mrs Winters. 'Do have a look. The back door is open.'

'Thanks.'

Dad stepped out of the back door and inspected the plants.

Mrs Winters turned to me.

To the side of the main room was a cupboard door. It was painted black and a piece of paper said 'KEEP OUT' on it. A chain at the top of the door held a bird's skull, its white beak protruding from the doorway.

'What's in there?' I asked.

Mrs Winters whirled around, extending her bony hands to grab my arms. Her grip was fierce, and for a moment, all I could see were her eyes, staring at me. Those eyes made the world around me disappear. They were hypnotic and bright with anger. She spoke in a voice that was little more than a whisper.

'There's one golden rule while you stay under my roof, boy. Do not, under any circumstances, try to open that door. Is that clear?'

I nodded, terrified.

'There's a good lad,' she said, suddenly smiling. 'I'm glad we understand each other.'

Frightened, I ran outside to be close to Dad. There were dozens of different plants, all in pots. Some had delicate orange flowers, or spiralling leaves that burst from an explosion of greenery. Each plant was labelled with their place of origin.

At the far end of the yard, leaning against a wall, was a moped. It was red with a gold stripe down the side. It had a long black leather seat and chunky, dark tyres. An exhaust pipe went along one side. I put my hand out to touch the handlebars.

'Cool,' I said under my breath.

'Wow, look at that,' said Dad, noticing the machine. He turned to Mrs Winters. 'Wouldn't have thought you were a moped rider?'

Mrs Winters gave a low chuckle. 'I'm full of surprises,' she muttered, winking at me. 'I suppose, James, you'd like a ride on this one day?'

'That would be awesome,' I said. Dad coughed. I looked at him. He had gone slightly pale.

'That might not be...' he said. But before he could complete the sentence, Mrs Winters interrupted him.

'Well,' said Mrs Winters, looking at me. 'If you are very good and do what you are told, you might get to try it out.'

I nodded.

'Well,' said Dad, 'I'm sure you two will get along very well. James has a lot of spirit, Mrs Winters. He does sometimes get into trouble at school. But his heart is in the right place.'

'I am sure,' said Mrs Winters, 'we will all get along famously. Won't we, Clarence?'

Clarence, as if agreeing, was rubbing around my leg.

'Great,' said Dad. 'We're leaving in a couple of days, and away for a fortnight. Right, come on James. We need to get home. Mum will wonder where we are.'

He looked at Mrs Winters.

'You do, of course, have all the usual documents, Mrs Winters? Insurance, health and safety?'

'Yes, of course,' said Mrs Winters, after a moment's hesitation. 'I will send copies to you right away.'

Dad nodded. He seemed a little uncertain as we left the house and returned to the car. I put on my seatbelt and looked out of the window. I looked back and saw Mrs Winters wave and smile.

'She's a funny old thing,' said Dad, chuckling.

'Yeah,' I said, biting my lip. I didn't say anything else. The old woman was a bit peculiar. And what was all the fuss about the cupboard?

But then I thought about the moped and the cake. Some things about staying with Mrs Winters might be really cool.

Chapter Five

'Line up everybody,' snarled Grindell. 'Come on, hurry up!'

Our class was going on a trip. Well, 'trip' wasn't exactly the right word for it. It was more of a 'walk around the corner', because Grindell had decided to take us to have a look at what he described as a place of local interest. 'We're going to study Gothic Architecture,' he announced. 'And the place we are going to is...'

The class waited for a moment. We held our breaths.

Maybe, I thought for a moment, we were going somewhere interesting and exciting. (Like Flamingo Park, which was this place with lots of awesome roller coasters with names like *The Diablo* and *Gravity Drop*. They also had Flamingos, but you couldn't ride on those. I tried, once. It was a very short ride and the Flamingo was pretty surprised to see me.)

But then Grindell completed his sentence.

'...St Cuthbert's.'

There was a low moan of disappointment from half the class.

'This will be part of our studies on sacred places.'

We'd been drawing mosques and synagogues. I'd said that the ground of Rigor Mourtice United and any Marshmallow Factories were sacred places, but for some reason Grindell had ignored my suggestions.

Beside me, Neville groaned.

'Sir,' he said. 'Can we go somewhere else? My Dad is the

vicar of St Cuthbert's and I have to go every Sunday and…well, I'm a bit sick of it.'

There was a general murmur of approval from the class. St Cuthbert's was the place to go if you wanted to have water splashed on your baby, or if you wanted to get married, or if you'd had enough of everything and decided it would be better to try being dead. It wasn't exactly the MOST exciting place. But then, the whole town was like that. As Neville and I often said, nothing ever happened in Rigor Mourtice.

But Grindell wouldn't listen.

'St Cuthbert's,' he said, 'is a site of historical significance and the visit will be educationally relevant. Now shut up stand in line!'

We trooped out of the school with our coats and our pencils, walking along the lane that sloped down to the church. I looked at my friend. He was frowning.

'Bad luck, Neville,' I said.

****

St Cuthbert's had a square tower and several stained glass windows. Grotesque stone gargoyles leaned out from the side of the church, with bulging eyes and flapping tongues. They looked like they wanted to be somewhere else.

In the churchyard were lots of old, dead people. They were lying under old rectangles of stone that said when they'd been born and when they'd died. Some stones had been worn smooth by the weather over hundreds of years. Some people had died in the seventeen hundred and something, which meant they must have been around when dinosaurs were alive.

'Hello, everybody,' said Rev'd Heavy. Neville's Dad was standing at the front door of St Cuthbert's. He was a tall man with a half-bald head. Sometimes he came to our school and did assemblies and told us to be kind if we wanted to get to heaven. Although, as I told Neville, I wasn't sure heaven was that much fun, really. If it was all about playing harps and singing, I wasn't that bothered.

****

Most of the time, I liked Neville's dad, except when he got strict and cross. If that happened, his cheeks went red and he shouted. For example, one time we were at Neville's house, playing *Vampire Zombie Lunatics*. In this game it was important to borrow Neville's mum's lipstick and draw red lines down the side of our mouths so we looked exactly like Vampires. When the blood / lipstick was in place, we ran around the house searching for a victim, who might be imaginary, or it might be each other, or it might be Neville's dog, Lester.

When the Vampire Zombie Lunatic finds the Victim they pretend to eat the victim, so there's a lot of fake snapping of teeth and fake munching noises and perhaps some Zombie burping, which is nearly the same as normal burping, but louder and more likely to happen at night. Then you could take turns to hide and be the victim. It was wicked. But it was a bit *too* wicked for Rev'd Heavy, who came out of his study and started shouting.

'I am trying to write a sermon!' he yelled. His face went pink. Then he said it was only a few days before Ankle Sunday or Palm Sunday or whatever it was.

'Boys, please,' said Rev'd Heavy. 'You are giving me a headache. Anyway, zombies are not pleasant creatures. Why don't you play something a bit nicer and quieter?'

'Like what?' asked Neville.

'Erm...why don't you play *Good Samaritans*?'

Neville nodded and we went upstairs. I told Neville there

was no way I was going to play *Good Samaritans* – it sounded like a lot less fun than *Vampire Zombie Lunatics*. But then Neville pointed out that the Good Samaritan story had a man who got beaten up really bad by the robbers on the highway. So then we played *Vampire Zombie Lunatics Meet The Good Samaritan*. I told Neville that the Good Samaritan would probably have to sacrifice his leg to keep the Zombie Lunatics happy and Neville agreed. He borrowed some ketchup from the kitchen to make it more realistic. But we might have used a bit too much because when Rev'd Heavy saw what had happened to the carpet he was very, very cross and took a long time to calm down.

****

'Good afternoon, children,' said Rev'd Heavy as we filed into the church. 'Welcome to our wonderful church building.'

Then he started going on about when St Cuthbert's was built and how old the tower was and who made the stained glass window. I was yawning my head off. After what felt like a couple of years, Rev'd Heavy gave us some sheets with a list of questions. We had to wander around the church and find the answers to questions like 'who died on 3rd May 1754?'

I wanted to write: 'A very very very fat man who'd eaten too many cakes in 1752 and 1753,' but Neville didn't think that was a good idea.

As we walked around, I noticed Mr Grindell had disappeared. I wanted to see where he was, so I tugged at Neville's sleeve, and we walked to the back of the church.

In a corner, looking at the wall with an intense expression in his eyes, was Grindell. I followed his gaze. High up, on the wall of the tower, and set inside a small alcove, was a pane of stained glass. Grindell carried on staring and staring at the glass, as if he was hypnotised by it. I looked up. It was hard to see what the picture in the window showed, but I could just make out an image of a red jewel, shaped like a diamond.

There were footsteps behind me. I turned to see Rev'd Heavy. He followed Grindell's gaze.

'I see your teacher has found our famous relic,' said the Vicar. He put a hand on Neville's shoulder as he looked up at the wall. Grindell hadn't moved.

'It is the most precious artefact in Rigor Mourtice,' he continued. 'The town council are very proud of it.'

'What is it?' I asked.

'You are looking at the famous Lunar Rose Window,' said Rev'd Heavy. 'It dates back to the eleventh century and is very valuable. According to a local legend, the window marks the location of a real diamond that is hidden somewhere nearby. Only trouble is, nobody has ever found it. There's an old saying, inscribed around the window. Apparently it provides a clue that will help somebody to find the stone.'

'What does it say?' I asked.

Rev'd Heavy smiled. 'Well it's written in Latin, of course, but a rough translation goes like this.' He briefly cleared his throat. 'Whosoever seeks the stone must search on the shortest night. But if the stone is pulled from its home...'

Grindell interrupted the Vicar to complete the rhyme.

'...it will bring disaster with a terrible might.'

Rev'd Heavy gawped.

'How did you know that?' he said, his mouth open in amazement.

'Oh, I must have read it somewhere,' Grindell said.

'I must say Mr Grindell,' said Rev'd Heavy, 'I'm impressed with your knowledge. The stone is said to have magical properties, of course. Needless to say, it has never been found.'

'Is it old?' I said, nodding at the window.

'Yes,' said Rev'd Heavy. 'It dates back eight hundred years, and remains in remarkable condition. Because it's so old, it's valuable. We try our best to keep it safe, but we can't afford a burglar alarm. We do get all sorts of strange people looking at it. But Lester tends to keep them away. If anybody goes in at night, he raises the alarm.'

Grindell nodded, a thin smile emerging on his face.

'Lester is your caretaker?'

'Oh no,' said the Vicar, chuckling. 'If only we could afford a caretaker! Lester is our family dog. A brown labradoodle. He's most fond of Neville, really. Lester barks very loudly if he hears anything.'

Grindell looked up. High up, near the tower, was a dark crack, about two feet long.

'That looks bad,' said Grindell.

'It should hold for a few years,' said Rev'd Heavy.

'Well,' said Grindell. 'Let's hope nothing happens to make the crack worse.' He nodded again at the glass window. 'A stunning picture. I'd love to take a closer look.'

Rev'd Heavy smiled.

'I must say, Mr Grindell, it is refreshing to find a local teacher who has a keen interest in history and culture. Do you have a special interest in unusual artefacts?'

'Oh yes,' said Grindell. 'I am very enthusiastic about the ancient world. Things were so much more straightforward then. They didn't mess around in those days. If somebody needed sorting out it was all very simple.'

He glared at me and Neville, sliding a long finger across his neck. Neville and I took a step back. Grindell turned away and began walking back towards the rows of pews. 'Now,' he said, 'shall we see how the other children are getting on?'

Chapter Six

'Here you go,' said Mum, pressing a pile of folded clothes into my arms. 'Take these upstairs, there's a good boy.'

Mum and Dad were about to leave for France. Piles of folded trousers, skirts and T-shirts were everywhere. Dad was messing about with computer files and sliding papers into a folder.

I put the clothes upstairs. I picked up my bag, which was packed with essential items:

- Two packets of Marshmallows (Utterly essential supplies. I'd wanted six, but Mum said two was plenty. She had no idea.)
- a football
- the latest edition of *Full Time* magazine
- a skateboard
- a battered copy of *The Black Island*, one of my favourite Tintin books
- my baseball boots

Mum has also packed some non-essential items like clothes, underwear and soap. Then I went down to the kitchen, where Emma was sitting at the table. We ate toast and Marmite and drank tea. The TV was on in the background.

'Right kids, after school today I need you to be home straight away,' said Dad. 'Your Mum and I have to leave for the airport at four o'clock. James, I'll take your things to Mrs Winter's house later this morning. Come straight home after school, right? No messing about. Your Mum and I have a plane to catch.'

****

'Right,' said Grindell, putting pieces of paper on each desk.
'Our first Science Test, Year Six.'

Oh no, I thought. Not Science. I looked at Neville. The night before, we'd spent two hours playing football in the park. Neville said we should get ready for the science test but I thought a kick about was a much better idea.

'Don't forget the Test!' said Neville. At home, I stared at my Science book. There were so many facts about cobalt and potassium and magnesium, I couldn't remember them all. It was hopeless.

'No talking,' said Grindell at the front of the class. 'There are ten questions. Now. Question 1. What colour is copper when it burns?'

Easy, I thought. I knew this one. Green-blue, I wrote down.

The next few questions were easy. Is wood magnetic? (Answer: No). What is the chemical symbol of Oxygen. (Answer: O2). But then it got really hard.

Question four: 'What is Newton's fourth law of motion?' I had no idea what this was about, so I wrote: 'Hamsters are faster than snails.'

Question five: 'What is smaller than an atom?' (Answer: 'A half of a third of a quarter of a baby ant's brain.')

Question six: 'How hot is the sun?' (Answer: 'Hotter than a holiday in the middle of an oven that's been on for a hundred years.')

By the time we got to question 7, I could feel panic rising inside me. I started to sweat. My eyes rolled. I felt anxious. It was the same reaction I had if I went without a Marshmallow for six days in a row.

Grindell ran through three more questions and then we had to swap papers. I swapped with Neville and we gave ourselves lots of ticks. We both got ten out of ten. It was all going really well, until Mr Grindell collected the answer sheets in. He stared at my sheet.

'Not only did you not do your homework, but you cheated in class!' Lucy Black gawped at me, as if to say 'James Small, you are capable of unimaginable evil. You are truly loathsome.' I tried to ignore her.

'I told you to behave,' said Grindell. 'Small and Heavy, the pair of you will see me after school.'

I felt down. I remembered what Dad had said about not being late.

'But Sir...!'

'See me after school!' Grindell bellowed. My heart sank as I realised this was bad news. Again.

****

At the end of the school day, Nev and I stood before Mr Grindell's desk as all the other kids went home.

'My Mum and Dad are going away,' I protested. 'I won't be able to say goodbye to them.' I felt sad.

'Well you should behave, boy, shouldn't you?' said Grindell, in a voice that said he wouldn't listen to my complaints. 'You two are a pair of useless, lazy toads. What are you?'

'A pair of useless, lazy toads, sir,' Neville said, his head hanging.

'And useless, lazy toads belong out there,' said Grindell, pointing out of the window at the pond. He marched us down the corridor, through the front doors, and onto the field. The ground around the pond was muddy and damp. The water looked cold and mean.

'Take off your shoes,' Grindell commanded.

Neville and I looked at each other nervously.

'I don't think...' I said, but Grindell repeated the command.

Neville took off his trainers, and stood in the grass in his socks. One sock had a hole in it. Neville looked miserable.

'And you, boy,' said Grindell, looking at me.

I took off my shoes.

'Take off your socks,' said Grindell.

We took off our socks.

'Roll up your trousers,' said Grindell.

We rolled up our trousers.

'Now get in the pond.'

'What?' I said, looking at Neville in alarm.

'GET IN THE POND!' yelled Grindell.

Slowly, I dipped a toe into the cold water. I put my foot down into the dark, soft, cold, squidgy mud. Then I put my other foot in. Lily pads moved as I walked into the middle of the pond. Neville followed me in.

'Now, repeat after me,' said Mr Grindell. 'We are lazy toads.'

'We are lazy toads,' we muttered.

'We belong in the pond,' said Mr Grindell.

'We belong in the pond,' Neville and I muttered.

'Now make a noise like a toad,' said Mr Grindell.

Neville and I looked at each other. I looked at Grindell, and hated him. He was the worsest, nastiest, most horrible man in the complete history of worse men.

Ever.

I made a noise like a toad. Neville made a noise like a toad. I looked at Neville. He was hanging his head. I watched a tear roll out of his eye. It was my fault we were in this mess. I felt terrible.

'I'm sorry, Nev,' I said. 'This is my fault.' Grindell had a smile on his face, and his lips drew slowly back to reveal his long yellow teeth.

'Stay there!' he ordered. 'For five minutes!' He turned and walked back to the school. There was only one thing in my mind as the cold mud squelched around my toes.

'I'll get you back, Grindell,' I thought. 'Just you wait.'

Chapter Seven

'You must be Mrs Winters,' said Neville's Mum.

'Hello dear,' said Mrs Winters, shaking Mrs Heavy's hand. 'A pleasure to meet you.'

Neville and I had finally escaped the pond. At last, Grindell told us to get out. We dried our cold, wet feet, then waited outside the school. Neville's mum turned up with the baby, who was sleeping in a pram, and, a minute later, Mrs Winters, riding her noisy moped.

Mrs Winters cooed at the baby. 'So sweet,' she said. She looked at Neville. 'Sorry I'm late, sweetheart,' she said. 'I was waiting for a delivery.' Neville looked relieved. Perhaps his Mum and Dad wouldn't find out he'd been in trouble.

'You're welcome to come to Lindsey's christening,' said Mrs Heavy. Mrs Winters beamed, said thank you, that would be lovely, then tossed me a small red and white helmet. Neville looked approvingly at the moped, but frowned at Mrs Winters. He was probably working out if she was a minor weirdo, a standard weirdo or a extra large weirdo with complex needs.

Part of me was nervous, too. She was friendly with Neville's Mum, but as I looked at the little woman with the wiry eyebrows and the missing finger, I remembered I had no idea who she was. I tried to focus on riding the moped.

'Hop on, James,' she said, then turned to Neville's Mum.

'Lovely to meet you, dear,' she said. 'See you soon, no doubt!'

I fiddled with the helmet but couldn't do up the strap. I asked Mrs Winters for help. She must have seen how sad I was looking.

'What's the matter?' she asked.

I told her what had happened. She shook her head from side to side.

'I don't like the sound of your teacher,' she said as she strapped the helmet under my chin. Then she turned in her seat. As she twisted the key in the ignition, I felt a buzz of excitement. She pulled back on the throttle. For a small machine it made a lot of noise.

'Hold on,' she yelled over her shoulder. I waved goodbye to Neville. My body lurched back as the moped pulled away. The sudden speed made me giggle.

A few minutes later, we were at Mrs Winters house. She showed me where she kept a key for the house: a red plant plot containing a drooping flower, a few feet from the front door.

'If you ever need to get in and I'm not here, you know where the key is,' she said.

The house smelt strange. A smell of dust mixed with the herbs that hung in the kitchen. By the sink was a jumble of cooking tools. Strange objects were everywhere: copper pans, battered recipe books, and dozens of small jars, each labelled with Mrs Winter's spidery writing. Some of the jars contained pretty strange things. I peered at one of them and read the label.

'Flies legs,' it said.

'Has this really got flies legs inside it?' I asked, holding up a jam jar. that seemed to hold tiny sticks with hairs on.

'Yes, dear,' she said. 'And very useful they are for certain spe-' Her voice suddenly stopped. She looked warily at me.

'Special recipes?' I suggested. I was hoping for some more cake after the treat I'd had a few days earlier.

'Yes!' she said, her eyes gleaming. 'For certain special recipes.' She took the jar from me, smiling, and placed it back on the side. 'Now, let me show you around. Oh! Your Mum wanted me to give you this.'

She handed me an envelope. I tore it open and read Mum's handwriting:

'James - Sorry to miss you. We had to leave for the plane. Be good for Mrs Winters. Don't get into trouble. Go easy on the marshmallows. See you in two weeks. Love, Mum and Dad x x'

I folded the note and followed Mrs Winters as she showed me around the house. A door at the side of the kitchen led to the yard where she kept more plants. Behind the kitchen was a tiny room, containing a small bed, an old cupboard and a washbasin. A tatty purple rug, depicting a crescent moon and some stars, lay on the floor.

The main room was the parlour. This contained a table and chairs, and two armchairs in front of a fireplace. Cushions lay on the chairs. On the walls, uneven wooden shelves were crammed with books.

'Your room is upstairs, dear,' she said. 'Have a look. It's the one that Clarence isn't in.'

I nodded, picked up my bags, and walked up the stairs. On the first floor were two small bedrooms. In one, curled up on a bed, was Clarence. He yawned, revealing sharp teeth and a pink tongue, then stared at me with wary green eyes. 'Stroke me and you'll soon be missing a finger,' he seemed to be saying.

I walked to the only other door on the landing. It revealed a tiny bedroom that smelt a bit funny. At one side, by the window, was a bed. It had a dark green blanket and a battered pillow that has been patched up in several places. There was just enough room for a bed and a wardrobe.

'Home sweet home, eh? I hope you'll be comfy, dear,' called Mrs Winters from downstairs. 'Your mum brought your things around.'

On the floor of my room was my suitcase and a cardboard box. For a moment I didn't move. My throat tightened up. I dipped my head and sniffed.

I sat on the bed and looked around the small room. There was a slightly musty smell. I was surrounded by pictures of a kid in a red hat driving a small red car. Next to the kid was a man with massive ears. He was grinning like a lunatic.

'Noddy,' I said, sighing. I felt like I was five. I thought of home, and pulled out the note from Mum and Dad and read it again. I'd never been made to stand in a pond before. Ever. I was sure that Mum and Dad would have something to say about that.

But now, they were a long way away. I thought of them at the airport, showing their passports to the security people, or boarding the plane. I hung my head and looked at the floor, suddenly feeling sorry for myself. I had a new teacher who I hated. And I was living with a strange old woman who kept legs of insects in jars.

And Noddy.

Chapter Eight

Mrs Winters house wasn't exactly ultra modern. There wasn't a microwave, or a DVD player, and not one computer anywhere. She didn't own a mobile phone and hadn't heard of the internet.

The windows were dusty. Doors creaked all the time. The tap in the bathroom was constantly dripping. Everything in Mrs Winters' house was ancient.

At first, this old house and its strange contents were a bit of a shot. But I soon started to feel at home. The kitchen always smelt of warm pastry. Every day, after school, Mrs Winters and I would make some new delicacy; soft flapjacks, luscious treacle tarts, crumbly apple pies, and raspberry trifles. We even invented a few new puddings, like 'James and Mrs Winters' toffee sponge', and 'rhubarb, pilchard and pickled onion pie'. I wasn't sure about the ingredients for that one. I tried to tell Mrs Winters to forget the rhubarb, but she wouldn't listen.

In the evenings, we'd light a fire and Mrs Winters would sit in her armchair and tell me tales of her travels around the world in search of ingredients for her special recipes. She told me wild tales of jungles and castles and mountains and caverns. She seemed to have been everywhere and done everything.

In the evenings, I'd look at some of her books. I'm not a big reader (takes too long, I'd rather be playing football or fighting aliens on Playstation), but there was no TV, so after I'd done my homework I investigated the bookshelves where hundreds of volumes leant against each other. They were great big things, and some of them must have been a hundred years old. Many of them seemed to contain recipes for strange herbal remedies, with long lists of bizarre ingredients. They had fantastic drawings of animals, insects and plants. One evening, as Mrs Winters was stirring stew in the kitchen, I took down a book from the top of the bookcase. It was large, with purple cloth covers and thick, yellowing paper. On the cover, in faded silver writing, it said:

Ye Olde Almanac Pertaining To The Control of Lycanthropes, 1776

I stared at the words, wondering what they meant. What were Lycanthropes? I didn't know. I turned over the cover and looked inside. But the pages were blank. The book was completely empty.

I looked at Mrs Winters for an explanation. But when she saw what I was holding, she rushed over and snatched the book from my hands.

'That's not for you!' she snarled, suddenly angry.

'I'm sorry, Mrs Winters, I...' I said. I was startled by her reaction. She told me sternly to go upstairs for five minutes. I tramped upstairs and sat on the edge of my bed. I could hear a door open and, half a minute later, close again, and Mrs Winters muttering something to herself. She called me down for tea five minutes later. We ate our tea. She acted as if nothing had happened.

****

One afternoon, a few days after Mum and Dad had left, Neville came over, and Mrs Winters took us out on the Moped. We scooted through the alleys of Rigor Mourtice and headed up to the Reservoir, where me and Neville took turns riding the machine. Neville wasn't sure at first, but after the first three crashes he got into it. Mrs Winters didn't seem to mind. 'Whoopsy,' she laughed, as Neville careered into a tree (broken branches, minor scratches) then took us for a circuit of the reservoir. Neville and I whooped with excitement as the moped circled the huge patch of sparkling water.

When we got back we had some tea at Mrs Winters. I watched Neville'e eyes widen as he entered the kitchen.

'Woah,' said Neville, looking at the collection of plants, herbs, pots and pans.

Mrs Winters grinned. We helped her make the tea: a massive pizza, covered in pieces of chicken, chunks of pink ham, triangles of pineapple and pieces of pepper. Cheese dripped off the side. On a plate sat a large chocolate cake. Neville licked his lips. I could tell he couldn't wait to try the cake.

Mrs Winters sat down and cut the pizza into large triangles. Neville and I tucked in.

'So,' she said, 'how was school?'

'Not good,' said Neville. 'Our teacher's a weirdo.' We talked about some of the strange things that had happened since Grindell arrived at the school.

'Hmmmm,' said Mrs Winters, chewing the pizza slowly.

'And what does he look like?'

I described him to her, told her about his eyebrows and hair and how he was tall and thin.

Mrs Winters nodded. She got up, went to the kitchen, and pulled a book from a drawer. She opened the book and held it up.

'Looks like this, does he?'

Neville and I stared at the book. On the page was a pencil drawing of a man who looked almost identical to Grindell.

'Wow...that's amazing,' said Neville.

'How do you know about Grindell?' I asked.

Mrs Winters tapped the side of her head. 'Never mind. Let's just say I have an interest in our Mr Grindell.'

Neville looked at her. 'Is he a friend of yours?' he asked.

Mrs Winters' face creased and her head tipped back. A loud cackle filled the room. Neville and I looked at each other.

'Oh no,' she said, wiping a tear from her eye as her laughter subsided.

'I have very different reasons for taking an interest in your teacher. Mark my words, boys, there is more to him than meets the eye. Do you want him to stay as your teacher?'

'No way,' said Neville.

'I wish he'd disappear,' I said.

'Well,' said Mrs Winters, 'I think that could be arranged. He can be overcome, with a little cunning on our part. But you have to help me.'

'What do we need to do?' asked Neville.

'Keep an eye on him. Make notes. Don't let anything escape your attention. Use your powers of observation, boys, hmm? And tell me what you see!'

Neville nodded. 'We'll do our best,' he said, licking pizza grease off his lips. 'Can I have some cake?'

'Manners!' said Mrs Winters.

'Erm...please?' said Neville.

Mrs Winters sliced the cake and placed it on two small plates, then handed them to us.

'Remember,' she said, 'keep an eye on him! Tell me everything he does!'

Part Two:

Don't Be Fooled By Appearances

Chapter Nine

The noise crashed through my sleep and woke me up.

I sat up in bed, listening. The sound was coming from the houses nearby. I tried to work out what it was. Then I realised: a dog barking. Something banged. There was a deep growl, and a vicious snarl. Then another bang. I heard a whimpering noise. Like somebody – or something – was in distress.

I got out of bed, pulled on my trainers, grabbed my torch, and went downstairs. Pulling open the front door, I peered outside. The moon hung in the sky. A breeze blew against my cheek. In the distance, a lonely owl hooted. Nothing moved. I put the door on the latch and stepped into the street. Quickly, I headed around to the alleyway where the noises had come from. A cat watched me from the top of a fence. The world slept.

I stopped for a moment, listening. At the end of the alley, I could make out a dark shape, and a strange snuffling noise. I held the torch in my hand and poked the light into the darkness, but whatever it was had already moved out of sight. My heart was beating fast. Something banged at the end of the alley. I started to run towards the sound, but I tripped and fell, the cold ground beneath my pyjamas. The torch left my hand, hit the floor, and span around so the light was shining in my face. In that moment, something moved nearby. I heard a whimper, and fast moving footsteps. Whatever it was, it had gone in an instant, knocking over a couple of bins that rattled in the darkness.

I bent down, grabbed my torch, and shone it around the alley. But it was too late. The thing, or things, had gone.

I stood for a moment, terrified. I tried to work out what I had seen. My heart was beating so hard I thought it would smash through my chest. I waited for a moment, then crept back to the house. Inside, Mrs Winters was snoring, the air whistling as she breathed. On her armchair, Clarence stretched, then curled up again. I went upstairs and got back into bed, waiting for my heart to stop pounding.

Chapter Ten

The next morning, the world seemed like a happier place. Mrs Winters was humming a song, her eyes shining in the morning light. The smell of fried bacon filled the air. Even Clarence seemed pleased to see me, purring as he rubbed around my legs.

'Good morning, James, dear,' said Mrs Winters.

A loaf of Mrs Winters' home baked bread sat in the middle of the table. I cut myself a slice as she put two rashers of bacon in front of me. Then I thought about what had happened during the night.

'Did I dream it?' I asked. 'All that crazy stuff from last night?'

'What happened, dear?' said Mrs Winters, looking at me over the top of her spectacles. I told her what happened. She listened with interest, then told me she wanted to ask a few questions.

I nodded as I chomped the bacon. Mrs Winters had produced a pencil and a piece of paper. She jotted down some questions, then looked at me over the rim of her spectacles.

'Right, here goes,' she said, a pencil poised in her hand.

'First question. Did the creature sound like a goat, pig, horse, sheep, cat, hamster or wolf?'

'Dunno. It was dark.'

'You can still hear in the dark?'

'Hmm. It's easier to hear in the daytime.'

'Did you get a close look at the creature?'

'No. It moved too fast.'

'Did the creature give off a smell?'

'Yes.'

'Did the smell remind you of any of the following: soapy water, chocolate brownies, bad toilets, unwashed dog, or the scent of lavender on a bright, clear October morning.'

'Erm...the scent of lavender on a bright, clear October morning.'

'Really?'

'No. I was joking. It was definitely unwashed dog.'

Mrs Winters peered over her spectacles at me.

'Please take this seriously, James,' she said. 'This is an investigation.'

'Right,' I said.

'Did the creature travel as slow as a snail, as fast as a bullet, or somewhere in between?'

'Somewhere in between. Snails take a long time to get anywhere and bullets travel at a maximum velocity of half a mile per second, making a total speed of 1,800 miles per hour.'

Mrs Winters looked at me again.

'How did you know that?'

'We did it in Maths the other day. After fractions. At least, that's what Neville told me. I spent most of the lesson daydreaming about marshmallows. I don't like school much.'

Mrs Winters blinked.

'Don't worry, dear,' she said. 'I was hopeless at school. And now look at me! And finally, would you say that this creature was after a cuddle or had a more sinister intention?'

'He had a more sinister intention.'

'You think it was a he?'

'Oh yes. There was no smell of perfume.'

'Well,' she said, looking at her notes, 'we can conclude that you came across a creature, possibly male, with sinister intention travelling down the alley at an uncertain speed, and that it smelt like unwashed dog.'

'And...?' I said.

'That's it,' said Mrs Winters, standing up to clear away the breakfast things.

'Oh,' I said. I felt disappointed. I was hoping Mrs Winters was going to come up with some remarkable conclusion.

'And,' said Mrs Winters, her voice drifting from the kitchen, 'that we are dealing with a Werewolf.'

I looked at her.

'What?' I said.

'You don't believe me?'

'I don't...' I bit my lip, unsure of what to say.

Mrs Winters raised an eyebrow.

'Do not be fooled, James,' she said. 'Mark my words, Werewolves are real, alright. They hide among us, disguised as normal people. You would never know if you passed one in the street. But when the full moon comes, they change into terrible, vicious creatures and cause all manner of mischief. And that creature is after something!'

'Why would a Werewolf want anything here?' I said. 'Nothing ever happens in Rigor Mourtice.'

'Well,' said Mrs Winters. 'Something is happening now. This is bad news for Rigor Mourtice, lad! A calamity! A catastrophe! A massive mishap! A supreme setback!' Mrs Winters rolled her eyes. She seemed to be enjoying herself.

'Are you a bit mad?' I asked.

She raised her eyebrows.

'Do I seem crazy to you?'

'Well, I wouldn't say you're totally normal.'

'Define normal.'

'That's easy,' I said. 'Normal is a person who likes football, Playstation and Marshmallows. Anyway, what was that about an investigation?'

'I never said that, dear.'

'Yes you did, you said: "This is an investigation." - I heard you.'

'No I didn't, dear. Anyway, it's time for school. You'd better clean your teeth.'

I held her gaze. I wanted an answer to my question.

Mrs Winters looked at me sternly. When she spoke her voice was a low hiss.

'James,' she said. 'Listen very carefully. There are some things I don't mind you saying to your friends, like what you had for breakfast, or your favourite football player, or what colour your bogeys are. But do not say a word to anybody about the conversation we just had. Is that clear?'

I nodded, but felt confused. Why was she being so secretive?

'Can I ask a question?' I asked. Mrs Winters nodded.

'How would you stop a Werewolf?'

'Ah,' she said. 'Good question. There are a number of techniques you can use. For example, you can tell them off. They will have to sit on the naughty step if they don't behave.'

'And does that work?' I asked.

'Oh no, dear. It's completely useless.'

'Right. And what are the other techniques?'

'My favourite is Werewolf Hypnotism.'

'That sounds better,' I said. 'How does it work?'

'It's a song I sing,' she said, 'based on an ancient melody from the tribes of Native American Indians. I'm using 'melody' in the loosest possible way. You have to look the Werewolf in the eye and recite the Hymn. It affects humans too. Want to try?'

'Yeah,' I said. I was intrigued.

'Okay,' she said. 'Sit still. Look me in the eye. When you start to feel dizzy, tell me. Alright?'

I nodded. Mrs Winters breathed in, breathed out, closed her eyes and stood in front of me. A low rumble came from her throat, quiet at first and then rising in pitch. The growls became loud, then quieter again. When she opened her eyes they were fixed on mine. Her voice rose in pitch.

At first nothing happened. I wanted to laugh. It seemed silly. But suddenly, the room seemed to tip onto one side. The noise coming from Mrs Winters filled my ears, like a roar. I could feel my eyes closing. I waved my hand and fell off the chair.

'Are you alright?' Mrs Winters said, a moment later. She was standing over me.

'Woah,' I said, slowly getting to my feet. 'That was...intense.'

I finished my breakfast in silence, grabbed my things and ran to school. It was all rubbish, I told myself. The hypnotism wasn't real.

But it took me a while to get the rubbish out of my head.

Chapter Eleven

'Where's Neville?'

Lucy Black shrugged in response to my question. I stood in the classroom, frowning. He was always at school before me. I went to my desk and sat down.

When Neville finally arrived, five minutes later, there were red rims around his eyes. He'd been crying.

'Nev, what's the matter?' I asked, as he wandered over to my table.

'It's Lester,' Neville sniffed. 'He's vanished!'

'Vanished?' I said. 'What do you mean?'

Neville started to cry.

'He was there last night and gone this morning,' he sniffed. 'I just want him back,' he sniffed.

I dug out an old tissue from my desk. It had some old bogey crust on it, and a bit of blood from when I'd had a nosebleed, and a bit of dust, but apart from that it was spotless. I handed it to Neville and he wiped his eyes. I put an arm around his shoulder. I hated seeing him upset.

We sat down at our desks. Children milled around, chatting and messing about. When Mr Grindell arrived, a few moments later, he called the register, then walked to his desk and picked up a copy of the *Maths Is Fun* workbook.

I hated *Maths Is Fun*. The front cover of *Maths Is Fun* showed a boy and a girl and a number '6' with a big smile on the face of the '6' and all three of them look deliriously happy, as if you might as well forget football, Playstation and Marshmallows, because Maths is all you will ever need to lead a fun, exciting life, which everybody knows is a massive lie. *Maths Is Fun* was full of fractions and percentages and decimals – the sort that made my skin turn green, and purple mucus come out of my nose. The name was wrong. A much better title would be: *Maths Is Pure Evil and Should Be Wiped Off The Face of the Earth Before It Makes Every Child Puke Out Loud.*

'Open the books at page 43,' he said, grumpily. 'Do the sums.'

****

'Hello boys' said Neville's mum, in the kitchen. Lindsey was in a bright yellow baby bouncer that was attached to a doorway. She bounced up and down, gurgling happily.

'Have you seen Lester?' Neville asked his Mum.

'Sorry, sweetheart,' she said, shaking her head.

Neville's face crumpled. He dipped his head and sniffed. I put an arm around his shoulder.

'Show me where Lester sleeps,' I said.

Neville led the way outside, into the yard. Lester's wooden kennel was by the back door. A red rubber bone lay, unused, in its doorway.

On the ground, in the soil of Mrs Heavy's garden, were two large footprints. I bent down to examine them. They had imprinted themselves into the soil.

Neville sighed. 'Somebody, or something, has been here, taken Lester, and run away!'

'Does your Dad lock the Church at night?' I asked.

Neville shook his head. 'Lester's our guard dog. He barks whenever there's an intruder. Well, he did, before...'

His voice trailed off. Neville, reminded of Lester's absence, dipped his head and sniffed.

'Why would anybody take Lester?' asked Neville, when we were back inside. He kept looking at the back of the kitchen door where Lester's lead was hung, as if he was expecting the dog to come in the room at any moment.

'He must be out there somewhere, James,' said Neville, sadly. 'He must be!'

Chapter Twelve

The next morning, Mrs Winters told me she was popping in to the school. We zipped around on the Moped as parents arrived with their children. Miss Lipps was shouting hello at Mums and pupils.

I swung my leg off the moped and walked past Miss Lipps. Mrs Winters was behind me. Children and parents turned to stare at the old woman. Part of me wanted to walk ahead, so people wouldn't think we were together. But that felt wrong. So I walked beside her as dozens of heads swivelled to see the strange old lady.

'Have a good day, dear!' said Mrs Winters cheerfully as we reached the main door. 'Which is your class? I might peak in through the window.'

'It's around the side,' I said. 'The window looks out on the playing field. Look for the drawings of places of worship.'

'Very good,' said Mrs Winters. I waved shyly and walked in to school. I got to class and sat down. Before a couple of minutes had gone by, children were laughing and pointing at the window. I looked up. At the window, Mrs Winters was peeking through the glass, her nose pressed up against it. She was so tiny that only her nose, eyes and hair could be seen. She rolled her eyes and waved. More and more children noticed. Mrs Winters was acting like a clown.

'Isn't that the woman that James Small's staying with?'

asked Archie Knight.

'What a weirdo!' said Dan Ricks.

Now I felt really embarrassed. I wanted to crawl up into a ball and hide. I put a hand over my face. She knocked loudly on the window as Mr Grindell came into the classroom.

I watched Grindell as he turned white. It was as if he had seen a ghost. His mouth dropped open and he seemed to tremble slightly.

'No!' he said. 'It can't be!'

'Nice to see you, again,' said Mrs Winters, loud enough to hear. 'I've got my eye on you!' Then she walked calmly away, her wild hair bouncing slightly as she did so.

Grindell blinked, breathed in and out, adjusted his jacket.

'That's enough!' he roared. 'Open your English books and carry on with yesterday's exercise.'

I opened my book but stole occasional glances at Grindell. He seemed to mutter softly to himself, and even dabbed at his forehead. Mrs Winters' sudden appearance seemed to have really rattled him.

Later that morning, Grindell was engrossed in his papers as we wrote out a passage on life in Ancient Britain. (I decided to make a few adjustments to my description. 'Life in Ancient Britain,' I wrote, 'was really smelly. I mean you thought things were bad when your Dad's just done a number two, well that was nothing like the smells in Ancient Britain. So they decided it was time for some plumbing.') Grindell kept inspecting a piece of paper, tapping it and frowning and muttering to himself.

'What's he looking at?' Neville whispered to me. I shrugged.

At break time, the classroom emptied. I went out into the playground with Neville, then pulled him behind the corridor door.

'What's up?' asked Neville. I put my finger to my lips. Grindell walked towards the staffroom. We waited until he turned the corner, then I pulled Neville with me and we crept back to the classroom.

'Keep an eye on the corridor,' I told Neville. He stood near the doorway to check if anybody was coming.

At the desk, I rummaged through the papers. Beneath the piles of Maths tests and maps of Africa, I found some photographs.

The photos showed a doorway and several windows in a large, old building. There was something vaguely familiar about it.

Then I realised.

'It's St Cuthbert's,' said Neville, shuffling through the pictures. There was one picture of the main doorway to the church, another of the inside of the rows of pews, and a third of the stained glass, high up on the side of the wall.

'Weird,' said Neville. 'Why is Grindell taking pictures of the inside of St Cuthbert's?'

Beneath the photographs of St Cuthbert's was a piece of yellowing paper, and a list, written in red ink. The writing showed strange, spidery letters.

'Look at this,' I said. Neville wandered over.

The list looked like this:

Ingredients Required
Dog Eagle egg (still warm)
Black Python – one eyeball
Lunar Rose (crushed)

'The Lunar Rose,' gasped Neville, pointing at the list. 'That's what the stained glass window in St Cuthbert's shows!'

'But what on earth is a dog eagle egg? And a black python?'

'I'm not sure,' said Neville. 'But I have a nasty feeling it's not good.'

I picked up the piece of paper. I wanted to show it to Mrs Winters. I folded it in half and was about to slip it into my pocket when a voice behind us boomed out.

'Give that to me.'

We span around. Grindell was standing in the doorway to the classroom, his eyes lit up with anger.

I gulped, took the list from my pocket and handed it to Grindell, who snatched it away.

'Leave that alone,' he snarled. 'And as for you,' he said, looking at Neville, 'I think I'll have a word with your father about this. He'll be interested to know about you poking your nose in places it shouldn't be.'

Neville's eyes blazed. I could tell he hated Grindell as much as I did.

'We'll…we'll…' stuttered Neville. He couldn't complete the sentence.

'Yes?' snarled Grindell. 'You'll what? Hold a meeting? Ask your father to say his prayers?' He curled his lip with sarcasm.

'We'll tell Mrs Winters!' yelled Neville, finally.

Grindell drew back for a moment. He paused. When he spoke his voice was low.

'Tell me,' he said. 'What do you know about your old friend?'

'I'm staying with her,' I replied. 'She's a child minder.'

Grindell smiled. 'A child minder! Hilarious! Perhaps when she's feeling more honest, she will tell you who she really is!'

He stood up, and waved the piece of paper that had the list on it.

'Keep your nose out of things that don't concern you. Both

of you. Or you may find yourselves in a situation that you can't handle.'

****

When I got to Mrs Winters house, I told her what had happened.

'Do you and Mr Grindell know each other?' I asked. She sighed. 'There is a lot of history between us,' she said. 'You could say we are old friends, although old enemies would be a better description.'

I asked her what she meant, but she told me to do my homework. I sat down at the table and clicked a pencil against my teeth.

Chapter Thirteen

It was Sunday. I was lying in bed, reading *Full Time* magazine and daydreaming about marshmallows when the smell of bacon drifted up from the kitchen.

'James!' yelled Mrs Winters. 'Breakfast! We need to be at the Church soon!'

I pulled on some clothes and stumbled downstairs. As I did, the phone rang, shrill and loud. I lifted up the ancient receiver as it was halfway through a ring.

'Hello?'

'James! How are you sweetheart?'

'Mum, hi! I miss you.'

'I know, we miss you too. How are things? Are you getting on okay with Mrs Winters?'

I hesitated. If I told Mum about everything that had happened, or mentioned Werewolves, she'd panic. She'd probably want to jump on the first plane home. My mouth flapped open, then closed again.

'Um,' I said.

'Are you alright?' asked Mum. 'Is Mrs Winters looking after you?'

'Yes, Mum,' I said. 'Everything is fine. The food is great. And...erm...the house is super.' I couldn't think of what to say.

'Are you washing each day?'

Uh-oh, I thought. Here we go. This is when it starts to get

really embarrassing, she'll be asking how many times I've been to the toilet.

'What's that, Mum?' I said, making whooshing noises in the sides of my cheeks. 'It's actually a really bad line.'

****

Lindsey was screaming. This wasn't surprising, as her Dad was pouring water down her face at the christening. I mean, if you were perfectly happy staring at the ceiling, and then your Dad poured water down your face at the end of October in an old church, in front of lots or people, you'd be annoyed, too! There was a ripple of laughter from the congregation and a few people made an 'aah' noise, as if torturing the baby by soaking it until it cried was somehow the cutest thing they'd ever seen. Grown ups are so weird.

As the laughter subsided, I felt something land on my shoulder. A small chip of stone had dropped from the ceiling above us. Several more bits of debris fell onto our heads and clothes. The laughter gave way to muttering as Neville's relatives brushed grey-white dust from their clothes and hair. People looked up, pointed, muttered.

'Where is it coming from?' asked Mrs Winters, picking a flake of stonework from her hair. She looked up, and my eyes followed hers. Far above us, in the church's ceiling, was the crack in the stonework. From where we were sitting, it looked like a streak of lighting threading its way over the wall. A small shower of dust and debris fell from the crack like powdered rain. Some of the congregation glanced up as Rev'd Heavy announced the final hymn. The music played, and some people were brushing hands over their clothes, trying to get the dust off.

I thought I could hear something thump outside the

Church, but nobody else seemed to notice, and soon we were near the door, waiting to get out, when something caught my eye.

'Look,' I said, nudging Mrs Winters. In the corner of the church, clambering up a statue of Dennis LePest, the founder of Rigor Mourtice, was Grindell. He was holding onto Dennis's nose with one hand, and pointing a camera at the Lunar Rose window, with the other.

Mrs Winters frowned and shook her head.

'There's no doubt about it, James my lad, he's up to something. And I reckon it's to do with the Lunar Rose!'

We sat for a while and listened to organ music as Neville's relatives filed out. Then we left through the main Church door, where Rev'd Heavy was standing. He didn't look very pleased to see us.

'I have received a complaint from a Mr Grindell,' said Rev'd Heavy, looking at me. 'He says he found you and Neville younger interfering with his things at school. Is this true, young man?'

'I…um…it's…err…' For once, I was speechless. But Mrs Winters came to my defence.

'James and Neville were acting under my instructions,' she said. 'I have asked them to keep an eye on Mr Grindell. The man is a menace. Did you know he has been taking photographs of St Cuthbert's?'

'I don't have a problem with that,' said Rev'd Heavy. 'We have nothing of value. And besides, I'm sure a cultured man like Mr Grindell…'

'Don't be fooled by appearances,' said Mrs Winters, sharply. 'Now, Vicar. Please think. What is precious in St Cuthbert's?'

'Well, the stained glass window. But I'm sure he wouldn't want to steal that…'

'No,' said Mrs Winters. 'Not the window itself, but it provides a clue. It shows where the Lunar Rose is buried.'

'But it's never been found,' said Rev'd Heavy.

'Not yet,' said Mrs Winters. 'But soon enough. Perhaps the next full moon, which is when Grindell will transform into a Werewolf.'

Rev'd Heavy stared. His eyebrows jumped. There was silence for several seconds. Then Rev'd Heavy's face split into a grin, he tipped his head back, and laughed.

'A Werewolf!' he said between loud guffaws. 'Ah! Brilliant! So funny. Priceless!'

Neville, Mrs Winters and I looked at each other. We weren't laughing. We waited for Rev'd Heavy's guffaws to slow down, then stop. When they did, Mrs Winters spoke calmly.

'Don't you believe in Werewolves, Vicar?'

'Certainly not,' replied Rev'd Heavy. 'But more to the point, I will not have my son getting into trouble for interfering with somebody else's property,' he spluttered. 'And I don't think James' mum and dad would like it, either. As for you,' he said, looking Mrs Winters up and down, 'it is quite clear you are not a positive influence on these boys. I do not believe in Werewolves, and I would appreciate if you stopped filling Neville's head with nonsense!'

His voice had got louder and faster. He was pointing a finger at Mrs Winters. For a moment, I saw a flash of anger in her eyes. But when she spoke her voice was steady and calm.

'I can assure you, Reverend, that nonsense has nothing to do with it. Mark my words, this town is in terrible danger! And Mr Grindell, I'm sorry to say, is not what he appears to be. I suggest we work together to overcome the present evil that is in our midst and work out what he's up to. So, Vicar, what do you say?'

Rev'd Heavy scowled.

'This is all rubbish!' he said, spitting the words out. 'I won't hear any more. You,' he said, wagging a finger a few inches from Mrs Winters' nose, 'are a bad influence.'

'There's no use in over-reacting, Vicar,' said Mrs Winters.

'I'm not over-reacting!' cried Rev'd Heavy, stamping his foot and spitting. His face had gone bright red. 'In the last few weeks, there's been nothing but trouble. Neville never normally gets into bother, but in the last few weeks, he's stayed behind at school, had to write lines, stood in a pond and now I've had a visit from his teacher!' He glared at Mrs Winters, and then at me, then put a protective arm around Neville.

'Why do you think Lester has vanished?' asked Mrs Winters.

'I...I don't know...' said Rev'd Heavy, uneasily.

'I think there's a good reason,' she said. Neville's face crumpled. He covered his face in his hand. I wanted to tell him things would be alright.

'Now look what you've done!' snarled Rev'd Heavy. 'Stay away from my son, the pair of you!'

Mrs Winters and I walked away from the Church. I felt sad. I didn't want to be in trouble. And I'd never asked to live with Mrs Winters, or for Grindell to come into our school. For a moment I wished that two other boys were caught up in this crazy mess. If only Rigor Mourtice could be quiet again, like it was before.

'Well,' said Mrs Winters, smiling. 'I think that went very well, don't you?'

Chapter Fourteen

Clarence rubbed around my legs, meowing. His saucer of milk was empty.

'We've run out of milk,' said Mrs Winters. 'I'll just pop up to the shop.'

I listened to her moped as it puttered away up the road. Apart from the occasional yowl from Clarence, the cottage was quiet. I made a cup of hot chocolate and sat down. I had homework to do: fractions. I sat in the parlour and tried to concentrate but my mind kept wandering.

I was sitting a few feet away from the cupboard that Mrs Winters told me not to enter. I looked around the room, taking in the piles of books, the herbs hanging in the kitchen, the bird's skull on the cupboard door. I started thinking about everything that had happened: her sudden move to the town, her interest in Grindell, her secretiveness. I stared at the door, and Grindell's question came back to me again:

'Has she told you who she really is?'

'Has she told you who she really is?'

'Has she told you who she really is?'

I got up, and stepped towards the cupboard. Why was Mrs Winters in Rigor Mourtice? Was there something she hadn't told me?

I stepped towards the door. There was a sudden yowl from nearby. I looked around. Clarence watched with accusing eyes, holding my gaze. He seemed to be telling me something.

Turning back to the door, I placed my hand on the handle, twisted and pulled. The door jolted open. Inside, the dark space smelt of cold dust. I stepped in, pausing as my eyes adjusted to the lack of light. At first I couldn't see what was there. I took a step deeper inside.

At the back of the cupboard, was a simple black table, with two items places on top of it. The first was a tall, battered black hat. The second was a book. When I looked more closely, I recognised it as the book with empty pages that Mrs Winters didn't want me to look at.

Next to the table, leaning against the wall of the cupboard, was a large broomstick, its dark bristles sticking out at numerous angles. The long handle of the broomstick had various scars and marks on it, as if it had been used a hundred times before.

My heart was thumping. My mouth was dry.

I gulped.

I stared.

I understood.

Mrs Winters was a witch.

Chapter Fifteen

No way, I thought. This is just a joke. Mrs Winters is playing a trick, she's having a laugh. And, anyway, I didn't really believe in witches, did I? They were things in movies, or Roald Dahl stories. They weren't *actually* real.

But there was something about the faded, ancient look of the hat (it actually had a couple of holes in it) and the simple look of the broomstick (a strip of old leather wrapped around the length of warped wood, bristles bound together at one end) that made me think it was true. They were so ordinary looking, like a scuffed pair of trainers. They were *real*.

'Found anything interesting?' said a voice behind me.

I turned around, taken by surprise. Mrs Winters was standing behind me, her eyes were half closed, her mouth tight with resentment.

'Mrs Winters,' I said. 'I...um...I was just...'

'I thought I told you not to go in here.'

She took a step towards me, her face half covered by the darkness of the cupboard. The kindness in her face had been replaced by something more threatening. She held up a hand and pointed with one long fingernail. Her jagged teeth were full of fury. Suddenly, she really did look like a witch.

'I'm sorry, I said, 'I...'

'Don't disobey me, child!' she hissed. Her face was a few inches from mine. I stammered. No words came out. I wanted to

75

be home, away from her, away from the old house with its strange books and ingredients and secrets.

She must have seen the fear on my face, because, after a long pause when all I could hear was her breath, pulsing in and out, her features softened.

'It's alright, lad,' she said. 'It's okay. I didn't mean to upset you. You might...you might as well know what's really going on.'

Chapter Sixteen

Ten minutes later we were sitting in front of the fire. Clarence was washing himself after a saucer of milk. Neither of us spoke as we stared into the flames. Mrs Winters was quiet and serious, the deep lines in her face gathered in a frown. She looked out of the window, and sighed.

'It's not easy living with secrets,' she said. 'You have to watch out all the time, cover your tracks, take great care. It takes its toll. Some nights I don't sleep too well.'

I nodded, unsure of what to say. I'd never been to the 'Witch Counselling for beginners' course.

She carried on.

'I suppose, James, you may as well know. My name is Audrey Winters. I am four hundred and seventy six years old.'

I gulped. Nobody was that old!

'There are things in this world that you do not understand, James,' she said, as if reading my mind.

'Strange things. Peculiar things. I am here on a mission, to defeat Grindell, before he causes terrible harm. I have spells at my disposal and I use the power of magic to help me. I've been known to wear a pointy black hat and ride on a broomstick.'

'So...erm...you're a witch?' I asked.

'Well, 'witch' is not a term we like to use in the family.'

'Family?'

'Yes. We're all related. We prefer to call ourselves 'Sisters of

Science'.'

'Sisters of Science?'

'Yes. It sounds so much nicer than calling somebody a witch. We've had so many image problems over the years. It's caused a lot of heartache in the Sisterhood. It's not all about broomsticks and cats, you know. In the bad old days, witches had to have cats. It was part of the rules. Even if you couldn't stand the things, you had to have one. And they had to be black. Some of the Sisters hated cats. There were rumours of animal cruelty – cats mysteriously falling from great heights or ending up in cauldrons. One of the French Sisters was known to make 'Gateaux de la Chat' and serve it to friends and family. A dreadful business. Caused quite a stir. In the end, cats became optional, and so did the colour. Clarence is my twenty-third ginger cat.' She sighed, and looked wistful, them picked up Clarence from the floor beside her and stroked his ears. He closed his eyes and purred contentedly.

'Things have improved greatly,' she went on. 'These days, if you decide you want a cat, you're given a cat allowance.'

'A cat allowance?'

'Yes. Vets bills are enormous these days. And broomsticks are optional. A health and safety nightmare. We kept losing Sisters who were flying around at night with no lights on and – bonk! – they'd smash into a chimney. No wonder so many of us have bent noses. So. Broomsticks are optional. Mind you, it's a wonderful feeling when you take off on one. The incantation is simple. You have to say: 'Broomstick glide, broomstick fly, I command you now to take to the skies.'

'It takes a long time to learn what I've learnt,' she said. 'All this...' She waved a hand at the bookshelves. 'It takes years to understand the world. Decades.'

'Mrs Winters, tell me about the book that has no writing in it.'

She shook her head. 'That's top secret, James,' she said. 'Sorry. You are too inexperienced to know of W.I.C.U.'s secrets. The book's contents can only be seen in special conditions.'

'What is W.I.C.U.?'

'It stands for Werewolf Incarceration and Control Unit. We are a secret organisation, dating back hundreds of years. Only a handful of people know of our existence.'

I stared at her. Then my eyes darted around the cottage. I wondered, again, if I should run away from her house. But where could I go? If I went to the Vicarage, Neville's Dad would never believe my story. I looked at the old woman. She was sitting in her armchair with Clarence in her lap, staring into the fire. Reflections of the twisting flames shone in her eyes. She looked tired.

Neither of us spoke for a while. I stared into the flames. We needed a plan if we were going to overcome the Werewolf. I wondered if Mrs Winters had thought of one. But would she tell me if she had? She was so secretive about some things. As I watched the fire crack and dance, I tried to think of what to do. Ideas raced through my mind, but each one seemed daft.

In the distance, St Cuthbert's bell was sounding. It was six o'clock. The evening service would finish in the next ten minutes.

At that moment, a totally ridiculous idea came into my mind. I got up and fetched my coat.

'I'm just popping out,' I said. Mrs Winters didn't reply. Her head had drooped to her chest and she was snoring gently. Clarence had curled up on her knee.

I went out, leaving the cottage as quietly as I could.

Chapter Seventeen

I walked alone. There was hardly a soul around. A sudden chill had descended, and a damp mist settled over the streets. The trees were mostly bare. Yellow leaves lay curled on the ground. The clocks had gone back, but nobody ever told me where they went. Pumpkins with garish faces began to appear in doorways and on paths, all crooked teeth and wide mouths.

When I got to St Cuthbert's, I crouched in the graveyard. It wasn't easy. The air was damp and I was getting colder. For once, I wished I was inside the Church. The evening service was about to end, and Neville would be ringing the bells.

I wasn't keen on hanging around the graveyard. It was creepy. I tried not to think about all those bodies lying beneath the grass, being tea for worms. In fact, I couldn't think what was worse, being tea for worms or being a worm and *actually* eating dead people. And what if there wasn't any ketchup? Then the taste would be *terrible*.

I was pretty bored so I ended up reading some of the gravestones of people who died from the time of the dinosaurs. There were spinsters and people who'd lived 'in this parishe'.

The church doorway opened, and a rectangle of light spilled onto the graveyard. Organ music came out of the building.

I watched from the gravestone as the people left the Church. Rev'd Heavy stood in the doorway, saying goodbye to his parishioners. The bells played and then, a few minutes later,

Neville left with his Dad. I waved at Neville but he didn't see me. I picked a small stone from the ground and skimmed it away from me. It pinged off Neville's ankle. He looked around, wondering what was there.

'Psst! I need to talk to you!' I said, trying to get his attention.

Neville looked warily in my direction, blinking into the gloom. I waved a hand. He looked nervously towards his Dad, still chatting to an elderly couple at the doorway to St Cuthbert's.

'Dad,' said Neville, 'I just...erm...need to look at some gravestones...erm...it's for our project...on ancient places...'

'Alright then,' said Rev'd Heavy, from the door 'Don't be long!'

Neville came over. We huddled by the gravestone.

'Listen,' I said. 'What if Mrs Winters is right? What if Grindell really is a Werewolf? Shouldn't we make a plan?'

'A plan?'

I nodded. 'If he really is a Werewolf, we need to think about what we're going to do. We need to work out how to stop him! And if we do, we'll never have to have another lesson with Grindell again!'

'We?' said Neville suspiciously. 'I'm in enough trouble as it is.'

'Come on, Nev,' I said. 'Give us a hand. If you help, Neville, I will make sure you get cake.'

'Hmmm,' said Neville. 'How much cake?'

'Piles of cake,' I said. 'Piles and piles. Huge mountains of cake. You'll need ropes and stuff just to get to the top of the cake. You'll be famous. People will remember Neville Heavy, the very first cake explorer in the history of the world!'

Neville blinked, then shook his head.

'Don't be silly, James,' he muttered. 'How can there be huge mountains of cake? And where will I eat it?'

'Let's worry about that when we've defeated the Werewolf,' I said.

'What we need, is something that will prevent the Werewolf from doing any more harm. Something we can drop onto the Werewolf that will stop him in his tracks. And I think I know what will do it.'

'What?'

'I'll give you a clue. It's very heavy and very loud.'

'Miss Lipps?'

For a moment, I had a vision of Miss Lipps toppling from the beam in the Church onto the Werewolf, flattening him.

'That's not a bad idea, actually, Neville. Miss Lipps, travelling at maximum velocity, would cause some serious damage. Lethal Lipps! I think I'll tell the people who make *Call of Duty* about that. But I don't think dropping our headteacher on to Grindell is the answer.'

'What then?' asked Neville.

I pointed to the top of the Church tower.

'Big Bill!' I said.

'What?' Neville's eyes widened.

'We lure the Werewolf under the bell, then we cut the rope so that the bell drops onto the creature's head. It knocks him out. Easy.'

'How are we going to do that?' asked Neville.

'Mrs Winters has this thing called Werewolf Hypnotism. She can use that to get the Werewolf under the bell. I'll crawl along the ledge and cut the rope holding Big Bill. It will drop down and knock the monster out. Sorted.'

'My Dad will not be happy,' said Neville, 'if we break the Church Bell. Not happy at all. He's always on about how great Big Bill is. But personally, I wouldn't mind if I never ever hear that stupid bell again. I am totally, completely, utterly sick of it.'

'Great!' I said, feeling good. 'We have a plan!'

'Let me get this straight,' Neville said, shaking his head in disbelief. 'Tomorrow night, everybody is going to be at the concert in St Cuthbert's. It's the day of the next full moon. According to you, Grindell is going to turn into a Werewolf. Mrs Winters is going to hypnotise him and make sure he's underneath the bell. You'll go up the tower and crawl along the beam that holds the bell, taking a pair of scissors. You're going to cut the rope and the bell will fall over the Werewolf. Then we hand him over to the police and we all go home.'

'Something like that, yes,' I said.

Rev'd Heavy's voice called out from the Vicarage.

'Neville! Come on! It's tea time!'

'Are you in?' I pleaded.

Neville bit his lip.

'Alright,' he said. 'I'll rig up a harness tonight, something that will hold you when you reach for the rope.'

I grinned. 'You're the best,' I said.

But Neville looked nervous.

'You better be right about this, James,' he said. 'Or we are going to look very, very silly.'

'Come on, Neville, don't be pessimistic,' I said. 'We've got a few hours to get ready. What could possibly go wrong?'

Chapter Eighteen

Strange dreams rolled around my head that night. Grinning pumpkins gnashed their teeth. A man in a suit had a bird's skull for its head. Miss Lipps was shouting for cake from the middle of a pond while a bell rang in the distance. I woke the next morning with a sense of unease. I tried not to think about this when I woke up, dressed, and ate my breakfast. Mrs Winters has issued a stern warning as I ate my toast: 'Be very careful around Grindell today,' she said as she poured the tea. 'It's Hallowe'en and a full moon. He will be at his most dangerous!'

Her words rang in my ears as I walked to school. I was good as gold. I kept quiet. I did my work. I didn't laugh or snigger or do any silly drawings or annoy Lucy Black. I kept out of Grindell's way. He was much more irritable than usual, snapping at children, or throwing their books across the room if they missed a comma. He paced up and down and scratched his skin. He looked out of the window every half an hour, as if he wanted the world to be dark. He looked like a man who knew something was coming.

****

After school, Neville and I went to help Rev'd Heavy set up St Cuthbert's. Miss Lipps was barking orders at children as they carried chairs to the Church. As Neville and I stepped outside, he noticed something on the wall near his Dad's house.

'Woah!' he said. He bent down by the wall and reached for something. He plucked a strand of brown wool from the wall.

'This is Lester's fur,' he said. He looked around, then walked towards the road. Another strand of fur was beside a road sign. And another thirty yards along the road, we found another one, snagged in a bush. Neville started to walk faster and faster, following the clues as he went.

We dodged past cars and bicycles. Neville ran down the road, and turned right into Silver Street. He came to a stop and began panting, his breath pulsing in and out. He stopped outside a tall house with a green front door. There were no lights on and the curtains were drawn. It was a gloomy looking place.

'I'm going in,' Neville said.

'What?' I said. 'Are you crazy? Wait!' But Neville was already crossing the road. I watched as he headed up the steps to the front door. He stretched out a hand to try the door. Then he reached inside his pocket and pulled out a strange looking tool, like a long, thin screwdriver.

'What's that?' I asked.

'It's for picking locks,' said Neville. He put his finger to his lips. 'You gave it me last Christmas, remember?'

I tried to think back. Christmas was ten months ago.

'Errr...I gave you a picture of you and me, made entirely from marshmallows.'

'Not that. The other present. The Burglar's kit? Remember?'

Neville and I went through this phase when we pretended to be burglars. This involved creeping around Rigour Mourtice and seeing if we could pinch anything. It was all going really well until we pinched a bollard on the road and then an old man fell down a hole where a gas pipe was being fixed. Rev'd Heavy and my Dad were not happy and said no more burglaring. I said maybe when we were grown up we could be burglars, and I gave Neville a kit called 'The Complete Burglar's Experience!' with a bag, a mask, a striped jumper and some black trousers. It also had a lock pick which Neville now held in his hands. He placed it in the lock.

'Nev,' I said. 'I really don't think this is a good...'

Neville ignored me, and twisted the tool one way and then another. There was a click and snap. He gave the door a tiny nudge and it creaked open. A line of darkness surrounded the edge of the door. I couldn't see past the crack.

'Bingo,' said Neville, grinning.

'You're not going in there, are you? We might get into trouble,' I said. I could feel my heart hammering.

'Stay out here if you like,' said Neville, shrugging.

'No,' I said. 'Wait. I'm coming with you. It's better if we go in together.'

'I'm coming, Les,' said Neville, and pushed the front door. It opened with a long, low creak. Neville stepped inside. A long, dark hallway lay before us.

I took a deep breath, and followed him into the house.

Chapter Nineteen

We stood in the hallway for a moment, waiting for our eyes to adjust to the gloom. There wasn't much light. A musty smell hung in the air.

To the left, a flight of broad stairs led up to the first floor. In front of us, and at the other end of the hall, was a closed door. There were two more doors to the right, but these were also shut. On a coat hanger beside the wall was a long green coat. It looked familiar.

'You know who that belongs to,' said Neville, nodding at the green coat.

'Oh no,' I said. 'That means this is Grindell's house.' A shiver rumbled up the back of my neck.

'Neville, I really don't think we should be here,' I said. 'Honestly. This isn't a good...'

Neville sneezed suddenly. The sound boomed around the house, echoing off the floor and walls.

'Must be the dust,' I said, running a finger along the wall.

'Gross,' said Neville, inspecting the dust that gathered on my finger. But I could tell he was determined to stay and investigate.

We crept slowly through the hall. The walls were dark brown. Ragged cobwebs clung to the corners of the ceiling. A spider scuttled across the floor. When was the last time this place had been cleaned?

'This place gives me the creeps,' I said.

Neville pushed open the door to the first room. Along the walls were large shelves holding old books, some of them covered in dust. There was a dark red carpet on the floor, and a solitary armchair in the corner. An ornate fireplace was set into the far wall. Neville wandered over to the books.

'Look at this,' he said.

'What?'

'There's a book here called *"The composition of human blood: properties and benefits."* And there's another one called:*"Extreme facial hair, how to deal with it and live an ordinary life."* And another one called *"Twenty new punishments for Small and Heavy."'*

'Very funny, Neville,' I said.

Back in the hall, Neville walked to the door at the far end. He pushed it open to reveal a small room with grey walls and a white floor. The air was cold and the floor was filthy. There was an old sink and a small table with a chair. To one side of the room was a large, metallic fridge that hummed softly. On a wooden table at the back of the kitchen were various bowls, test tubes and glass vials. A shelf on the wall held glass containers of various sizes and shapes, some thick with dust. There were numerous glass containers marked 'magnesium', 'potassium', 'cobalt' and more. A large brown sack on the floor seemed to contain a mixture of chemicals. I tried to remember something Grindell had said in class about the qualities of potassium and magnesium, but I was distracted by a burst of barking from outside. Neville rushed over to the window and peered out.

'Look, James, it's Lester! Look!'

We looked out of the window. In the yard, tied to an old chain that was fixed into the wall, was Lester. His mouth had been muzzled, preventing him from barking.

'But I don't understand,' said Neville. 'How did he get into Mr Grindell's house?'

I shook my head. My mind was racing as I tried to understand all the things that had happened.

The creature in the alleyway.

The disappearance of Lester.

And now we'd found him at Grindell's house.

It was all too weird.

'We need to get this open,' said Neville, tapping against the back door.

'How are we going to do that?' I asked.

'Allow me to help you,' said a deep voice behind us.

Chapter Twenty

I whirled around to see Mr Grindell standing in the doorway. His body cast a long shadow that fell across us. A hideous smile spread across his face. His lips were peeled back to reveal large yellow teeth. But there was something weird about his smile, as if he didn't really mean it. I froze to the spot, unable to talk or move.

Grindell's eyes narrowed.

'This is private property,' he said in a low voice. 'You have no right to be here.'

'What is my dog doing here?' Neville said, pointing to the window. His voice was low and determined.

'There was a dog on the loose two nights ago,' said Mr Grindell. 'He seemed to be lost, so I thought I would do the right thing and provide him a home. You wouldn't want him wandering the streets, now, would you?'

'Lester wasn't on the loose,' replied Neville. His voice was quick and loud. 'He was fastened on a rope, tied to the drainpipe in our yard,' said Neville, walking up to Grindell and staring at him. 'You took him away because you want something from the Church. And you muzzled him so he wouldn't be able to bark!'

Grindell bent forwards until his face was level with Neville's.

'You shouldn't be in my house, boy,' he said. 'Trespassing is a crime, you know.'

'And so is stealing other people's pets,' said Neville. 'That was a nasty thing to do!'

Grindell twitched with anger, his lip curling into a sneer. He raised an arm and clutched Neville's shoulder, then brought his face close until their noses were almost touching.

'The animal is safe,' said Grindell. 'Which is more than can be said for that old bat you've been hanging around with.'

'Mrs Winters? What do you mean, she isn't safe?'

Grindell's lip curled in disgust. 'She's dealing with things that she cannot control. She thinks she'll overpower me. But she won't. Just like the last time we met. And the time before that. For a woman who's been around a long time, she has a lot to learn. Now, beat it. Take your revolting little dog, and leave.'

Grindell took a key from his pocket and twisted it in the door. Outside, he bent down to untie Lester, who was making whining noises behind his muzzle. He seemed desperate to see Neville.

Lester ran to Neville. Neville removed the muzzle and Lester barked happily, licking Neville's face and hands. His tail wagged excitedly. I was glad they were reunited, but I wanted to leave.

'Come on Neville,' I said. 'I think it's time to go.' Neville didn't need to be told twice. As we pushed past Grindell he snarled at us, opening his mouth and baring his teeth. A low growl came from his throat.

Suddenly, I was really scared. It wasn't his threat to call the Police that bothered me, it was Grindell himself. He wasn't just a teacher, and he wasn't just a man. There was something about him that was unreal. I knew, in my gut, that I couldn't trust him – not because he was a teacher who gave out weird punishments, but because I didn't know who he was. I shivered at the thought. I wanted to get out of there. I turned to look at Neville.

'Come on,' I said, my voice more urgent this time.

'Lester? What's up?' Neville was looking at his pet. Lester was baring his teeth, ears back, growling.

'What's the matter, boy?' said Neville again. He bent down to stroke the dog, but Lester had started to bark wildly.

'I think something's bothering him,' I said. Then I froze. Something had changed in the room. I could feel it. The atmosphere was different. As Lester carried on barking, getting more and more hysterical, I slowly turned.

Grindell was looking out of the window, fixed on the moon. There was a strange look in his eye. He was transfixed, his body still as a rock.

He didn't budge.

He didn't blink.

He carried on staring at the moon. And then his eyes slowly turned a milky white colour. Soon they were like two pale marbles. There was a tiny twitch in Grindell's neck, then another in his cheek.

And another.

Soon his skin was rippling with twitches, as if something inside of him was trying to break out. His eyes bulged. His head was thrown backwards, as if he was suffering from some sort of seizure. His arms and legs twisted about in spasms. His head thrashed from side to side and his breathing grew faster and louder. Grindell's limbs became longer and thicker, splitting the clothes he had been wearing. Hairs sprouted from his head and hands. His ears were large, pointed things. Thick brown hair streamed away from his head and covered his cheeks. Long, yellow claws sprouted from the ends of his fingers. He had grown two feet taller in a few seconds. With a last, terrible cry, the transformation was over.

Grindell was no longer a man.

He was a Werewolf.

The creature swayed from side to side for a moment, as if getting used to being in its changed state, then looked slowly around, licking its lips. A line of saliva hung from its upper teeth. Cruelty shone in its eyes and a deep growl rumbled from its throat. Then it raised its head and let out a howl that filled the house.

'Neville,' I said, backing towards the door. 'We better get out of here.'

Part Three

There's Absolutely Nothing
To Worry About

Chapter Twenty-One

Getting two panic-stricken boys and a dog out of a house should be easy. But we were so frightened by what we'd just seen that we kept knocking into each other, a flurry of arms, legs and paws and a tail. I panted. Neville puffed. Lester barked as his paws scrabbled against the floor. We burst out onto the street. Behind us, another terrible howl went into the air.

'Look! Mrs Winters!' panted Neville.

The old woman was pulling up to the house on the Moped. Under her left arm was tucked the broomstick.

'I warned you, James!' she said, scowling. 'I told you not to go near him! On today, of all days! Hurry up, climb on. There's no time to lose! We must reach the Church before he does!'

I climbed on the moped and clutched on to her. Neville, with Lester tucked under one arm and barking madly, got on behind me and the Moped roared along the road, the cold wind whipping at our ears.

I looked behind us, and glimpsed a dark shape running down the steps of Grindell's house, then scamper along the road behind us. It was fast. A shiver ran down my neck.

'Mrs Winters,' I said. 'He's coming. Can this thing go any faster?'

We roared through the streets of the town.

'Neville and I have a plan!' I yelled at Mrs Winters.

'What's that?' she shouted.

'You do the hypnotism and get him to stand under the Church Bell. I'm going to cut the rope that holds the bell. It should fall down and knock the Werewolf on the head.'

'You'll have to be quick,' yelled Mrs Winters. 'The spell doesn't always last long.'

St Cuthbert's was ahead of us. Mrs Winters pulled on the brakes with seconds to spare. Beneath us, the road had a silver sheen of frost.

'Ice!' yelled Mrs Winters. Seconds later, the bike span wildly. Mrs Winters yelled as she lost control. Neville wailed. Lester howled. The Moped skidded, hit the edge of the pavement outside the Church, and Mrs Winters went flying over the handlebars. Neville, Lester and I all toppled to the ground. I grazed my chin on the concrete, and Neville rubbed his arm.

'Mrs Winters?' I said. Neville peered at her. She was out cold.

Chapter Twenty-Two

The Handbook had fallen open on the road. Its pages fluttered in the breeze. Above us, the full moon shone in the sky. As a cloud slid past it, the moon glowed a little brighter. The letters on the page became clearer.

'Look!' said Neville. As we stared at the book, writing began to appear on the pages, tiny characters that looked like they'd belonged to another time.

'You can only read it in the full moon,' said Neville.

I flipped through some more pages with Neville peering over my shoulder. We examined diagrams showing different parts of a Werewolf's body. One picture showed the jaw of a Werewolf and its different teeth. On another page, I saw something that looked familiar. There was a small drawing of a diamond, embellished with red ink. I stared at it, trying to remember where I'd seen something like this before. Then I realised what it was.

'Look. It's the Lunar Rose,' I said, nodding up at the window above us.

My eyes scanned the text.

'Whosoever wishes to create diabolical pestilence can do so by locating several extraordinary ingredients. The following ingredients must be located: a dog eagle egg, the eyeball of a black python and the Lunar Rose. Grind them into a fine powder, then stir them together and pour on a cup of boiling sour milk.

When the whole mixture is bubbling, allow to cool and place in a vat of warm mud. Wait for several days. When the potion has turned green it is thus complete. One drop of the potion, placed in a drink, will be enough to poison a man, woman or child. Whosoever uses this magic recipe could unleash a terrible force into the worlde, turning normal souls into gnashing, vicious werewolves. The location of each ingredient is not to be told to any soul. Guard this secret with your Life.'

'So,' said Neville. 'Now we know what he's up to. He's trying to assemble the ingredients for a potion that will turn normal people into Werewolves. He could infect thousands of people, even millions!'

Lester began barking wildly. I turned and looked down the street. A figure was lumbering down the road towards us.

'He's coming,' Neville said. 'We've got to warn everybody! Quick!' Neville and Lester headed for the door to St Cuthbert's.

I bent down and picked up Mrs Winters, who was still unconscious.

I called to Neville. We stood on either side of Mrs Winters, and lifted her up. We dipped our heads under her arm, scooped up the book and the broomstick, and carried her into the Church.

Chapter Twenty-Three

Neville slammed the Church door shut, then slid the metal bolt across. Mrs Winters murmured something as I placed her on a chair at the back of the Church. She wasn't looking great, but I felt relieved that she was making some noise. I placed the book by her side then turned to look at the congregation.

The concert was about to begin. The place was full; it seemed like the whole of Rigor Mourtice had turned out.

'Good evening everybody, and welcome to our annual Concert,' said Rev'd Heavy, his voice loud in the empty Church space. 'I am especially pleased that...Yes? What is it, James and Neville? I'm not sure this is the time to...'

'Shut up, Dad!' said Neville, running to the front. 'Our town is in danger! There is an evil presence among us!'

'Yes, um...' I said. 'Somebody in our town is not who they say they are. They hide a dark secret.'

The people in the pews muttered to themselves. A man in the fourth row said he'd always wanted to try ballet. A woman near the back confessed that she enjoyed two kit kats a day.

'No,' said Neville. 'That's not what we mean. What we mean is...erm...that...there is somebody here who is, in fact, a danger to Rigor Mourtice.'

'Neville,' said Rev'd Heavy, 'you can't go making pronouncements like that. Who are you talking about?'

Neville looked at me. He gulped.

'Mr Grindell,' I said 'is a Werewolf!'

There was a moment of stunned silence as my voice echoed around the building. Everybody stared at each other in amazement. Somebody sniggered. Somebody else chuckled. And then the whole congregation exploded in laughter.

I bit my lip. In that moment, I knew what everybody was thinking. The laughing faces of parents and children all said the same thing: Neville Heavy and James Small were off their heads. Bonkers. Loopy.

'He's on his way here, now. It's a full moon and we've just seen him turn into a Werewolf.'

The laughter had got louder. One man clutched his sides. A woman near the back wiped a tear from her eye.

'That's quite enough,' said Miss Lipps, glaring at us. 'The idea that Mr Grindell is some sort of mythical beast...it is ludicrous!'

Rev'd Heavy turned to the congregation. 'I do apologise everybody,' he said, smiling nervously. 'And now, the school orchestra are going to play 'For All The Saints In Heaven Now Abundantly Abounding'.

Miss Lipps, trying to carry on as normal, gestured to the musicians to carry on. They picked up their instruments and began to play, the violins and piano and oboes filling the church. But before they could play a note, something thumped the Church door. Then again. Then again. Within three knocks the door was rattling. The fourth blow buckled the lock. With the sixth blow the left door was knocked clear and swung uselessly on its hinge. The crack that ran up the wall spread a few inches, and then a few more.

Everybody gasped at the figure that seemed to fill the doorway. For a moment he stood motionless, then stepped forward into the building. Candlelight flickered on his face.

For Rev'd Heavy, the shock was too much. He stared. He gawped. He pointed.

'Lord in Heaven...'

But it was all he managed, because he fainted, falling back onto one of the chairs. Mrs Winters had stood up and was walking, a little unsteadily towards the creature. She turned to me and nodded. I gulped. It was the signal for me and Neville to move.

'Let's go,' said Neville. We ran towards the tower. Neville produced the key from his pocket and rattled it in the lock, his hands trembling. He yanked the door open, and a whiff of cold air came from the tower. At the side of the door was the head of the gargoyle that had fallen off the Church's exterior. The head leered at us with protruding teeth and wide eyes, as if warning us not to go any further.

At the doorway, I looked behind us. Mrs Winters had got to her feet and was standing, a little unsteadily, in the main aisle of the Church, ten feet from the Werewolf, who sniffed the air.

A low, rumbling growl came from its throat and for a moment it swayed from side to side. Then it threw back its head and let out a terrible howl.

Chapter Twenty-Four

Neville and I ran up the steps of the tower. It took us about twenty seconds. We were out of breath when we came to the top.

'Have you got the harness?' I asked, panting.

Nev nodded, and showed me a plastic bag.

'I put this here last night, after our chat in the graveyard,' he said. It gaped open enough to show a length of rope with a wooden handle attached to Lindsey's bright yellow baby bouncer.

'A skipping rope?' I said. 'And a baby bouncer? Are you nuts? If I don't die from falling to the floor, I'll die of embarrassment!'

'Nobody will remember this when we're heroes!' said Neville. 'It was the only thing I could find. Come on, you'll be fine.'

But I could tell he wasn't sure.

I shook my head. 'This is crazy,' I muttered, as I peered out of the doorway that led to the beam and Big Bill. Beneath us was the church floor. I gulped. It was a long way down.

St Cuthbert's had erupted into pandemonium. Parents and children fled, dropping their carol sheets on the ground. Babies were crying. Children were crying. Adults were crying. Miss Lipps was shouting even louder than usual. Desperate to get away, some of the children hid under the pews.

Mrs Winters leant forward, raised a hand and beckoned the creature to come near. The Werewolf, eyes locked on Mrs Winters, crept slowly towards her, his mouth opening a little as he approached. My stomach ran cold with fear. I didn't want Mrs Winters to be eaten.

'Put it on,' said Neville, thrusting the harness at me. I tried to strap into the thing as fast as I could.

'You look great,' Neville said as I stood there in the baby bouncer. He was smiling.

'Very funny,' I said. He held the bike chain in his hand, a metal clip one end. He fixed it to the harness and passed me a pair of scissors.

'Okay,' he said, as the metal teeth clicked together. 'You're good to go.' I looked out of the hatch. Below me, the candlelight gave out a pretty glow as the congregation hid among the pews, as far from the Werewolf as they could go.

I pushed myself out on to the beam, and crawled forward, clutching the scissors between my teeth. The beam was just wide enough to support my body. I crawled along. It was surprisingly warm up there. The heat from the candles had drifted up to the top of the building. My heart was smashing away. It seemed like a long, long way down.

L   ying flat on the beam, I reached underneath for the rope with my right hand. I took the scissors from my teeth, my hand shaking with fear. I felt the blade touch the rope and I started to saw into the fabric. Spots of ancient dust rose into the air, whirling around like tiny, dirty fairies.

Below me I could hear Mrs Winters raise her voice as she addressed the crowd.

'Nobody move,' she said. 'Stay where you are.'

And then she began to make a strange, low, humming noise.

'She's doing the hymn of Werewolf hypnotism!' I hissed to Neville.

'Not very catchy, is it?' said Neville.

The humming continued for a short while.

'Okay,' he said. 'Mrs Winters is moving him into position under the bell. Everything's going to plan!'

I tried to nod but it wasn't easy. The dust was swirling more and more around my face and nose. I could feel a sneeze begin somewhere inside my nostrils. I looked below. The Werewolf had succumbed to Mrs Winters hypnotism trick. She was slowly moving forward, the Werewolf in front of her, shuffling backwards. He was almost directly beneath me.

I twisted around the beam and looked at the thread. Pieces of rope had snapped off. It was over half way cut through. As I watched, another piece of twine snapped loose.

'She better hurry,' I hissed at Neville. 'This rope isn't going to hold forever!'

'She's almost there,' he whispered back. 'Get ready. I'll tell you when.'

I lay back on the beam and reached again for the rope. I put the blade against the rope. I breathed in. More dust swirled around my eyes.

'Okay,' said Neville. 'Do it now!'

Clutching the scissors in my hand, I sawed the rope as fast and hard as I could. I was sweating from the heat and the effort and nervousness. The sweat was running into my eyes. I pulled my hand back, put the scissors in my mouth, and reached for a handkerchief.

'He's right there!' said Neville. 'Let it drop! Now! Now!'

I felt dizzy. The dust was making my eyes water.

And then it happened.

I sneezed. As the 'atchoo' came out of my nose and echoed

around the building, my mouth opened. And the scissors fell.

'You've got to be kidding,' I said.

'I don't believe it,' said Neville.

The scissors twisted through the air for a moment, twisting as they fell, like some metallic angel that was tumbling to earth. In that moment, they became something terrible, because I knew they were heading straight for the Werewolf. Our plan wouldn't work. The scissors bounced off the Werewolf's shoulder, and fell to the stone floor with a clatter.

'Oh no,' said Mrs Winters.

The spell had been broken. The Werewolf, no longer in a state of hypnosis, shook his head, growled, and looked up. He let out a ferocious roar. For a moment he seemed to glance up at the small window at the top of the tower. His muscles tensed for a moment and then he launched himself into the air, springing to the top of the pulpit, looking up to the bell.

He was only eight feet below us. Then I gasped. He was reaching up to the space beneath me, his claws closing around the rope.

Chapter Twenty-Five

'James!' hissed Neville. 'Let's go!'

'Easy for you to say, Nev,' I said. 'A werewolf is beneath me, I'm lying on a beam, and I've got a ridiculous harness attached to my body.'

'Come *on*!'

I got to my feet and turned around. The bell was swinging a little from where I had tried to cut the rope, frayed pieces of fabric sticking out from the side.

As I turned, something caught my eye. Through the dust, something was gleaming. For a moment, I couldn't understand what it was. Then I realised. Behind me, the full moon shone through the window at the back of the Church. The light of the moon passed through the building towards the small window before me.

In the centre of the small stained glass window, the red diamond was gleaming from the heart of the full moon. The diamond, catching the light, sent a thin red beam from its centre and beyond the Church tower. I could see the line of crimson light as it stretched above the town's rooftops, beyond the church. It was hard to see where it went.

'James, hurry!' said Neville.

I squinted through the window. I could just make out a small beacon glowing in the distance where the beam settled on the landscape, half a mile from the Church.

'What is it?' asked Neville.

I stared into the distance. Something shifted beneath the moonlight, and very close to where the red light was. A twinkle, a shifting light. Then I knew. The Lunar Rose was buried near the reservoir.

But I didn't have long to think about this. Beneath me, a hairy paw reached up to the beam, long claws digging into the wood. I jumped over the paw and hurried towards Neville, who reached out his hand. I clasped his hand in mine and hurried back inside the tower. We ran down the stairs as fast as we could, almost tripping over as we hurried.

We reached the bottom of the tower and pulled the door back. I was in such a hurry that I knocked over something that was on the floor. Looking down, I saw it was the head of the gargoyle. It toppled back, preventing the door from closing.

'Forget it,' said Neville. 'We've got more important things to worry about.'

Panting at the doorway, we looked up. Above, the Werewolf was swinging on the bell, growling as it swayed from side to side. As we looked, the rope started to give way. The thread was close to snapping. As the last threads of rope came away, the Werewolf sprung into the air, three claws digging into the wood. He heaved himself onto the beam.

And then the bell fell from the beam.

We stood there watching it, Neville and I, as it dropped to the floor of the church with all the grace of a large hippopotamus. It hit the ground with a tremendous thump, giving out a long, low DOOOONG as it landed. The noise echoed around the walls of the building and filled our ears.

Looking up, we could see the monster squatting on the beam. He was crouching on all fours, straining to look out of the window at the line of red light that streaked across the town.

For a moment, he was quite still as he stared out of the dark. And then, with astonishing speed, he sprang from the beam, landing a couple of feet from Mrs Winters, reached out, and slashed at her face. His paw swiped through the air.

'Mrs Winters,' I cried. 'Look out!'

The old woman tried to move back, but she wasn't fast enough. The Werewolf's claws sliced through her skin, leaving three long marks upon her cheek.

Mrs Winters looked stunned. For a moment her eyes locked onto the Werewolf's. The creature growled at her, and he seemed to smile for a moment. And then, with a leap and a bound he sprang over the pews, scurried over the floor and through the ruined doorway. He went into the night.

I went over to Mrs Winters.

She opened one eye, looking at me warily.

'He's got me, James,' she said. 'This is bad. It means I'll become infected.' She frowned as she touched her cheek. The blood gleamed on her fingers. Her eyes rolled in her head.

'I'm seeing double,' she said. 'If I hadn't fallen off the Moped, I would have been more effective with the hypnotism, and maybe he wouldn't have hit me.'

'What can I do?' I said.

'Try to stop him! I'm sorry boys. I'm not going to be much use to you. You can use the moped. And you better take this. You might need it.'

She handed me the broomstick. I felt its rough wood inside my palm. I swallowed. I wasn't sure if I was brave enough to face the challenge before us. As if reading my mind, Mrs Winters said. 'Be brave, James. You can do it.'

'Thanks,' I said softly. She nodded at me, a smile on her lips and a steely look in her eye. 'Now go.'

With the broomstick in my hand and Neville at my side,

110

we ran for the Church door when Rev'd Heavy shouted at us.

'Boys!' he yelled. 'It's not safe! Stay here!'

For a moment, Neville and I stood there, caught between two choices. We could be sensible. Or we could have an adventure.

It was Neville that nudged me through the door.

'What are you waiting for?' he said.

I gulped, and followed my friend into the darkness.

Chapter Twenty-Six

The Werewolf ran down the street. At the corner, he bent down and picked up something, but I couldn't see what it was in the gloom. Then he was off, scampering away from the town. He soon vanished from view.

'The moped!' I said to Neville. 'It will help us catch up with him. Here, take this.'

I pushed the broomstick into Neville's hands, then clambered on. I flicked on the headlight and a pale circle of light lit up the street in front of us, picking out the Werewolf in the distance. I turned the ignition key and pulled back the throttle.

'Hang on!' I said. We dashed through the streets. Apart from the moped's noise, the streets were quiet and empty. The town was deserted; everybody was cowering in St Cuthbert's, trying to keep out of danger and away from the Werewolf. And here we were, following him. This is crazy, I thought, as the moped raced on.

At the edge of Rigor Mourtice, we started to climb the thin lane that wound up the hill, then onto the steep grass bank that led to the edge of the reservoir. After the sweat of the church and the danger of balancing on the beam, part of me was glad of the cool night air and the firm ground beneath my feet. But my heart was thumping hard as we came to the edge of the reservoir.

'Look up there!' said Neville. He pointed to where the beam

of red light came to rest. It was focused on a patch of wet earth, twenty feet in front of the water's edge.

A few minutes later, we were crouching in the grass near the rim of the reservoir. A cold wind snapped around our heads. Catching my breath, I looked down the hill at the town. I could just see the faint light of pumpkins glowing in the windows of houses. Their faces were orange grimaces in the dark.

'Stay down!' hissed Neville. 'Don't let him hear us!'

A short distance away, we could see the Werewolf, digging his claws in the earth, heaving away great sods of mud and grass into the air over his shoulder and into the air. He was like a digging machine as he burrowed through the earth. We were close enough to hear his panting. After a minute, the bits of flying earth had become chunks of stone, whistling through the air. One landed at our feet. Neville bent down to examine it.

'He's through to the harder ground,' said Neville, holding up a piece of rock. 'But how's he going to...' Neville's eyes widened.

The Werewolf was crouching in the grass. He pulled something from a bag. Above us, the full moon illuminated the scene.

'I thought I saw him get something in town,' I said to Neville. 'But what is it?'

'It's a sack. Was there something like that at Grindell's house?' said Neville. We watched as the Werewolf emptied the contents of the sack. A fine powder spilled from the sack and filled the hole in the side of the earth.

'That looks like the stuff we saw in his house. Oh no. Magnesium and potassium. You know what that makes?'

'A very bad sandwich filler?'

'Explosives, James, explosives! He's going to blow a hole in the hill so he can get the Lunar Rose. But if it damages the reservoir, the water will pour down the hill. The town will be devastated!'

'It's at times like these I wish I'd listened to what my Dad used to tell me,' I said.

'What did he say?' asked Neville.

'I don't know, I wasn't listening.'

The Werewolf shuffled backwards, placing something on the ground. He was edging closer and closer to where the three of us were. In the darkness was a snapping sound and a sudden glow of yellow light. The Werewolf's face was illuminated, his mouth slightly open, his pupils shrinking from the sudden glare of a lighter. The creature bent to put the lighter on the piece of string. It flared up, quickly threading towards the stash of explosives.

'Hit the ground! Now!' said Neville, pushing me nose down into the ground. I spluttered, spitting the cold mud from my mouth.

I looked up for a moment.

And the world turned white.

Chapter Twenty-Seven

The blast that roared around us drowned everything out. The world was soaked in heat and light. The earth rumbled and shook. For a moment, I thought an earthquake had begun, or a volcano was erupting.

Above our heads, massive chunks of rock flew through the night sky, landing on the hillside with heavy thuds. One landed a few feet from where we lay, while smaller bits of stone and earth showered down on top of us, pinging off our heads, shoulders and backs.

'Crumbs,' said Neville. 'That was louder than Miss Lipps on a bad day. What's the Werewolf doing now?'

Lines of dark smoke from the explosion made it hard to see.

'He's disappeared.'

I looked up and peered through the smoke.

'There he is!' The Werewolf emerged from the hole that had been blown into the side of the hill. Something gleamed in his hand. He held it up to the light of the moon, entranced by the reddish gleam that came from the jewel. His eyes seemed to sparkle with delight.

'Oh no,' I said. 'He's got the Lunar Rose. Now we're in trouble. If the blast went into the hillside, it could have fractured the side of the reservoir.'

The rim of the reservoir was a smoking crater, a crack ten feet long was letting water tumble down the hillside. As I watched, the crack got wider.

'We're about to get wet,' I muttered. 'I think we'd better run!'

We got up and turned, ready to go down the hill. But within seconds, it started. A great, foaming swell of water began rushing down the hillside. It slipped past our feet like a wide, wet snake, glistening in the moonlight.

'Woah,' I muttered, as our shoes and boots became flooded. 'It's cold.' My voice rose. But before I could complain any more, the water had risen to our ankles and then, seconds later, was up to our knees.

'Where's the broomstick?' I said.

'It was just here,' said Neville, looking down at the ground.

The water was up to our waists now, pushing us downhill. I couldn't stand up where I was. Neville held on to me, desperate to stay upright, but his body swayed backwards and forwards. Neville tried to reach for the broomstick but it wiggled out of his reach. The water pushed it one way and then the other. A moment later it had been lifted up and sailed past, swept along by the swell of water that was now rushing down the hill. The Werewolf was running down the hillside, one hand gripping the Lunar Rose tightly. He was taking great leaps as the water lapped around his ankles, but he couldn't outrun the deluge that was at his heels. Finally, he lost his balance, and the water splashed against his body.

'What are we going to do?' Neville asked, panic in his voice. 'We're going to get swept away.'

He was right. The water was pushing us down the hill. It was now around our waists. My feet were being swept away from the ground as the water rushed faster and faster, carrying everything with it. The boulders that had smashed into the earth were now twisted by the flow of the water. Ahead of us, a tree trunk, ripped from the hillside, was being swept along.

'Grab on to the tree,' said Neville. We grappled with the tree trunk, our hands slipping on the damp surface. I clambered on, exhausted, then turned and reached for Neville's hand. The tree was hurtling down the side of the mountain, the town rushing up beneath us. If we carried on this course, we'd smash straight into the bridge. And that would only mean one thing.

'We're going to die!' said Neville, his teeth chattering with cold and fear. 'And it won't be nice!'

'Neville! Don't give up! We're not finished yet! Look! The broomstick!' It was several feet away, and half submerged. The bristles pushed through the surface, like a hedgehog learning to swim.

I leaned out as far as I could. The cold water took my breath away. I stretched out my arm, my fingertips reaching for the broomstick. It was getting closer. But it was beyond my fingertips. I reached out as far as I could, trying to keep my body flat in the water. Finally my fingers curled around the wood.

'Right, climb on Neville,' I said. 'Let's see if this thing works.' I looked towards the bridge. There wasn't much time.

Chapter Twenty-Eight

The Werewolf, swept along in the current, was coming closer and closer to our tree trunk. He wasn't exactly swimming. In fact, he appeared to be half drowning in the waters. Spluttering noises came from his mouth as he desperately flapped his arms. I remembered what Mrs Winters said about them being terrible swimmers.

He was really close now. With a desperate lunge, he grabbed hold of the trunk with one paw. His fur, now slick and spiky with the water, made him look like a bedraggled dog. I raised one foot and brought it down, hard, on the paw of the creature. His eyes widened as he roared with pain.

'You want me to save you?' I asked.

The Werewolf blinked, then nodded.

'Then do exactly as I say,' I said, holding out my hand. 'Give me the stone.'

The Werewolf bared his teeth.

'Give me the stone and I'll save you,' I said again. 'You better hurry. You haven't long to make up your mind.'

The Werewolf dropped the stone into my palm. I passed it to Neville, who placed it inside his jacket. I bent down, and extended the broomstick's end towards the creature. Grabbing it, he scrambled up onto the tree trunk. Towering over us, water dripping from his mouth, I kept him at bay by poking the end of the broomstick into his stomach. The Werewolf snarled as his paws tried to catch the broomstick. Tiny fragments of broomstick bristle were swiped away, whistling past my ear as they flew. The Werewolf was lunging past me, looking at Neville. He wanted the Lunar Rose.

Neville and I backed to the edge of the trunk. Ahead of us, the bridge was rushing closer.

'We'll be crushed! Smashed! Squished!' moaned Neville.

We approached the edge of town. I could see the dark outlines of the houses in the October night. Neville ducked as the Werewolf's massive paw whizzed through the air. I suddenly felt angry, and slammed the broomstick down on the Werewolf's head. The force of it seemed to make him dizzy. He tottered around the trunk.

'Neville, climb on the broomstick,' I said. 'Quick, while he's still hesitating!'

We shuffled onto the broomstick. I tried to recall the incantation that would make it take off.

'How does it go, now?' I said. 'Mrs Winters told us, didn't she? Let me think. Ah yes. Broomstick glide, broomstick fly, I command you now to take to the...' I couldn't remember the rest.

The Werewolf shook its head, snarled, and came towards us. The bridge was in front of us. Foam crashed of its walls, as if the bridge itself was salivating, hungry for something to munch. I didn't want to be its supper.

'What was the last word? Flies?' I said. 'Cries? Cherry Pies?'

'Skies!' screamed Neville in my ear. 'For God's sake, skies!'

'Ah nice one, Nev,' I said. 'Spot on. Here goes nothing.' I cleared my throat and spoke in the most commanding voice I could muster.

'Broomstick glide, broomstick fly, I command you now to take to the skies.' For a second, we waited. Nothing happened.

'Try again!' said Neville.

I ran through the incantation again. But before I got to the end, we lurched backwards as the broomstick shot into the air, almost vertical, our feet an inch or two from the side of the bridge. For a moment something seemed to be dragging it down, then it sped up, taking the breath from my mouth. All we could do was hold on and hope for the best. The wind roared in our ears and our stomachs turned with the sudden velocity. I closed my eyes.

'Woaaah!' yelled Neville.

'Hang on!' I said as we sped upwards.

I waited for a moment. My heart was hammering and I was breathing hard. Neville was talking to himself. I could feel him shivering next to me.

'Neville?' I said. 'Are we still alive?'

'Think so,' he said. 'I don't want to open my eyes.'

'Me neither,' I said. 'But we can't stay up here all night.'

'You look first,' he said.

'No, you,' I said.

'No, you look first, James,' he said. 'I'll give you my secret supply of chocolate.'

'You haven't got a secret supply of chocolate,' I said.

'Um, I do actually,' said Neville. 'It's just very small.'

'Look,' I said. 'Throw in a bag of marshmallows, and you've got a deal.'

Neville went quiet for a moment.

'All right,' he said. Then there was a pause.

'James,' he said in a small voice that told me he was worried.

'What's that hanging from my foot?'

I felt sick as I slowly opened my eyes. We were high above the town, coasting along in a wide circle. We seemed to be rotating above the river. Below us the streets were empty and still. I shifted in my seat. Broomsticks were not a comfortable way to travel. The October air and the cold reservoir water were making both me and Neville shiver.

I turned around and looked down.

'Oh no,' I said.

'What?' said Neville. 'What is it?'

'Um,' I said. 'The Werewolf. He's holding onto your leg.'

Neville looked down and shrieked.

'Stay calm, Neville,' I said. 'We can do this.'

But I had no idea how.

The Werewolf, dangling from Neville's leg, let out a howl.

Chapter Twenty-Nine

My head swam with ideas as we flew above the town. Neville was gripped by fear. He blurted out noises, not words.

'It's alright, Neville,' I said. 'I've got an idea. You keep the broomstick steady. I'll reach down and untie your shoe.'

'Yeauurrgrgggh,' said Neville.

'Okay, hold tight.'

I pulled my legs up and wrapped them around the broomstick. Then I lowered my body down so it was beneath the beam that Neville was sitting on. I stretched out my arm. Neville's shoe was just out of reach, and on it, were the Werewolf's claws. His eyes looked at me, burning with anger.

'Nev,' I shouted. 'You need to lift your foot, okay? Just a little. Raise it up.'

Neville whimpered above me. I reached out my hand and began tugging at the edge of Neville's shoe. The Werewolf grunted angrily, adjusting its grip. I told myself not to look in its eyes. I could feel the shoe loosening a little, but it was tight to budge.

Think, I told myself. Think, James, think. Then I realised.

'Neville, have you got the Lunar Rose.'

Neville made a strange noise.

'Pass it down to me.'

The Werewolf's eyes seemed to widen in interest.

I looked up. The moon cast a silver glow on Neville's face. His lips trembled with cold and fear. He reached into his pocket and pulled out the Lunar Rose, passing it to me.

I held the stone in my hand and waved it in front of the Werewolf.

'You want it?' I said. 'Come on then. It's right here!'

'Whatever you do, Neville,' I said, 'keep your foot still.'

I put my fist, with the edge of the stone showing, on the top of Neville's foot. The Werewolf slashed wildly at the space. Each time, I moved the stone so he couldn't reach it. His claws swiped at the edge of Neville's shoe, slicing a line three inches long.

Neville yelped with alarm.

'Hold still, Nev,' I yelled, then looked at the Werewolf. We were above the school now. Below us, the pond was illuminated by the moonlight.

'Come on, little doggy,' I said, letting him glimpse the Lunar Rose once more. 'Come and get it.'

The Werewolf growled and slashed again with his arm. His claw caught Neville's shoe and the split widened again. I reached down and tugged at the shoe. It came away. As it fell, I caught a look of surprise in the Werewolf's eyes as he fell through the air, tumbling down. It took him three seconds to reach the ground. There was a faint sound of a splosh as he landed in the river. His body disappeared in a plume of white foam and fell beneath the surface. There were a couple of bubbles, and then the water closed around the monster. He was gone.

I swung my body around the broomstick, punched the air with my fist and whooped.

'Yahooooooooooooooo!'

Neville looked down. He managed a whimper of delight and smiled.

We circled around the scene a couple more times, to make sure the monster was gone. The grey and white foam of the tumbling waters carried everything with it. Grindell was gone.

As the broomstick descended, I looked down on the town. The water smashed into the bridge, making the centre of it crumble. Huge lumps of the bridge tumbled into the torrent as the water streamed through the town, flooding streets and doorways.

Chapter Thirty

Below us, the water seemed like some ferocious creature, a mixture of white foam and brown sludge. I remember seeing a programme on TV about a Tsunami in another country, and how a coast was ruined by the force of the water. This was really bad news for Rigor Mourtice.

'If the water hits St Cuthbert's,' said Neville, 'the place might not survive! And everybody is inside. Come on, hurry!'

I pointed the broomstick in the direction of St Cuthbert's and it plummeted from the sky. Seconds later, we were hovering five feet above the ground, next to St Cuthbert's.

'We need to get everybody out,' said Neville, pointing to the church. 'Come on!'

We jumped off the broomstick, water sloshing around our ankles. Waves were slamming into the butcher's at the top of Hill Lane, knocking bricks off the corner, then ricocheting into the Post Office, before sliding towards the church, falling against themselves in loud slaps.

I pulled the door of St Cuthbert's open and three hundred faces looked at me.

'James! Where is the creature?' asked Rev'd Heavy.

'He's gone,' I said. 'He was carried along by the water. There's no time to explain. You have to leave here, straight away. The reservoir has been damaged and the water's heading this way.'

A weird creaking noise came from the walls. Rev'd Heavy's

face went pale as he looked up. A dark line was climbing the Church wall.

'Oh my Lord. The cracks...'

He stared at the water gushing in the entrance. He turned to the congregation.

'Hurry everybody, through the south transept. There is a door that leads outside, the path goes up the slope to the school. You will be safer on higher ground. Go now, and may the Lord Preserve us!'

Children and parents and grandmas started to move through the church in a confusion of noise. Somebody was crying. One of the grandmas said the last time Rigor Mourtice had been this exciting was when the May Pole fell over in 1974.

I looked around the Church for Mrs Winters and saw a small figure huddled in one of the pews.

'Are you alright?' I asked.

'You follow them,' said Mrs Winters in a thin rasp. 'I'll keep the doors closed as long as I can.'

I hesitated. 'Will you be alright?' I asked.

She nodded gravely, then waded over to the front door of the church, her clothes darkened by the water. The tiny woman was already half submerged beneath the water as she leaned against the door, trying to stop more water from entering the building.

Neville and I followed the crowd of people as it tried to leave the Church. It was painfully slow. There was nothing Neville and I could do except wait. And then something fell into the water.

'Oh no,' said Neville, looking up at the ceiling. Lumps of white stone were dropping from the ceiling. There was a low creak from above us, as if the building itself was unhappy.

'We haven't got long,' I shouted. 'Hurry, everybody! The

church is crumbling!'

There were twenty people left inside, fumbling towards the door as the water gushed in, rising all the time. Something creaked in the tower.

And then it came. The pressure broke open the wall, poking a jet of water into the building, like a hose. At first the crack was about two feet long, but within seconds it was spreading, making the wall buckle and bend. The wall gave way, great lumps of brickwork and stone falling into the water, making a small cloud of plaster.

I peered through the haze to where Mrs Winters was standing, her back to the door, her head and neck just above the water. Another minute and she would be beneath the water. My stomach flipped over in panic.

The wall of the church began to surrender, the crack getting wider and wider as the deluge poured in. I knew we didn't have long. My heart thumped within me. I started to push the last few people through the door. Behind me, huge chunks of stone were smashing into the water. Cold, muddy liquid leaped up to splash my face.

Ahead of me, the queue of people were scrambling for the steps that led up the slope towards the back of the school. There were sobs of relief as people staggered to safety, above the level of the water.

I turned back. The church was in chaos, the water overwhelmed the candle sticks, tipping them over until the flames went out, one by one, the smoke rising above the waters. The Church was going dark.

'Mrs Winters!' I screamed. But my words were obliterated by the sound of the stone wall falling into the water. The final candle went out, and the place was overtaken by darkness.

'No!' I yelled. 'No! No!'

Chapter Thirty-One

A hand pulled me through the door and away from the church.

'James,' said a voice. 'Leave it. There is nothing you can do now. Come on.'

'Dad!'

I was relieved to see him, and glad when he put his arm around my shoulder. But I wanted to stay there, yelling into darkness, hoping to save Mrs Winters. I cried as Dad pulled me away.

'Let go! I have to help her!' I tried to break free of his grip, but he wouldn't let go, and half carried me, half shoved me away from the church.

I closed my eyes and howled. I could hear voices around us, and a sudden intake of breath from the crowd. Behind us, there was a roar of noise. I opened my eyes and looked down the slope at the church, which had started to fold in upon itself, the walls caving in like a sandcastle when the tide tumbles over the beach. The tower, leaning over, surrendered to gravity and fell to the ground. There was a strange whooshing noise as the walls met the water, and the high tinkle of glass shattering. A huge cloud of grey dust rose up. I stood there, shaking with the cold and wet, and watched as the building turned to rubble. Dad's hand was on my shoulder. Then I turned, buried my face in his chest, tears running down my face.

Chapter Thirty-Two

It was a long night. Bedraggled families huddled together in the school hall, shivering. A pool of mud formed at the entrance. Some of the adults made cups of cocoa. Everybody was in shock at what had happened.

I stayed with Mum and Dad and Emma in one corner of the hall, next to Neville and his family. Mum and Dad kept asking me questions about Mrs Winters and Mr Grindell. Mum wanted to know why I hadn't told her about what was going on. I told her I didn't really know what was going on. 'Things just...sort of...happened,' I shrugged. Mum gaped and shook her head. There was a lot of muttering.

Dad said I'd been really brave and he was proud of me, but I kept thinking about Mrs Winters. Was she dead? Was she alive? 'We need to find her,' I told Dad.

'Yes,' he said, his arm around my shoulders, 'but right now, it's too dangerous. Let the emergency services do their work.'

I drank from a cup of cocoa, feeling the warmth of the cup inside my fingers. Dad laid his coat on the floor. I lay down and closed my eyes. Exhausted by everything that had happened, I slept.

I woke several hours later, cold air on my face. Mum and Dad were bundling me and Emma into the car. I looked out of the window. The water was still several inches deep, but it was going down. We passed the place where St Cuthbert's used to be, now a big mound of rubble, with half of the church tower standing up amid the ruins. I listened to the hiss of the car moving through water as we drove on.

****

The doorbell woke me up. I'd spent the night at home, in my own bed, under my own Rigor Mourtice United duvet. It was a relief to escape from Noddy. Home smelt normal and familiar. Everything was where I'd left it. There was a thin layer of dust on the windowsill and bedside table, but apart from that everything was the same. I lay there for a moment, relieved to be home, and wondering if the last two weeks had been some sort of nutty dream. Then I remembered. Mrs Winters. I got up, and yanked open the curtains.

Below, the streets of Rigor Mourtice were alive with a small army of police officers and firemen. Other people wearing high visibility jackets were talking into walkie-talkies. A camera crew had turned up to film the scene.

Downstairs, the front door bell rang again. I heard it click open.

I could hear Mum's voice as she answered the door.

'Mrs Small?' said a voice.

I could see a large, bald man with a thick moustache and quick eyes.

The fat man held out his hand. 'Harry Williams,' he said, smiling. 'I'm the Chief Constable of Noirshire. We'd like to ask you a few questions,' he said.

We went in the living room and I sat on one of the sofas opposite the two policemen. The chief constable spoke first.

'Right, James, tell me everything you know.'

****

'Have you found Mrs Winters?' I asked, almost an hour later. I'd been through my story about five times. There were a lot of questions.

The Chief Constable frowned. 'Is she missing?' he replied.

I couldn't believe it.

'You are kidding me,' I said. 'She was in St Cuthbert's when it collapsed. Please, help me to find her.'

For a moment, the Chief Constable hesitated. He looked thoughtful. His tongue tapped three times against his teeth.

'Alright, lad,' he said. 'Come with me.'

****

The dust had settled. The water was still and had collected in great pools around the ruined building. Rev'd Heavy was picking through the rubbish, shaking his head and muttering. He hadn't shaved and his hair stood up around his head. His trousers were caked in mud. In a plastic box beside him, the Vicar had put things that he'd salvaged. There was a bent candlestick, five or six sodden hymnbooks, and a few broken pieces of stained glass.

'James,' said a voice behind me.

It was Neville.

'Who's this?' asked Neville, glancing at the Chief Constable.

'He's in charge of local Police,' I said. 'Any sign of life? Have you seen her?'

'I've been here half an hour. At first there was no noise. But I heard something a few minutes ago. Over there.'

He pointed to the pile of rubble that used to be St Cuthbert's. 'It sounded like somebody coughing.'

The Chief Constable shouted orders to several policemen, who began hauling away pieces of stone. Walkie-talkies crackled with life. The Chief Constable spoke to a man in a dark suit who called several offices over, pointing to the tower.

I bit my lip and surveyed the scene. Rev'd Heavy was picking through the rubble, shaking his head and muttering. I watched as he bent down again and when he stood up he was holding a section of a stained glass window. There were tears in the Vicar's eyes. I felt bad. Although Rev'd Heavy and I didn't always see eye to eye, I hated to see him like this. He looked like a man whose whole world had fallen apart. He nodded at me.

'I should have listened to you and Mrs Winters,' he said. 'She was right all along.'

Behind me, the Chief Constable was already calling men over.

'Get the digger and the fork lift ready,' he told one of his men. 'And six men with shovels. Hurry!'

I watched as the men went to work. The digger moved pieces of the church wall and turned over pieces of broken pews. A couple of the men clambered into the centre of the ruins. One of them waved his hands.

'Cut the engines,' shouted the Chief Constable.

There was a moment of silence. Everybody waited and listened.

And then:

'Do hurry up!' called a weak sounding voice from the remains of the church tower. 'My cat will be starving!'

Tears filled my eyes. Mrs Winters was alive! I looked at Neville. I wanted to climb in straight away to reach her, but the Chief Constable put out a hand.

'Sorry, lads,' he said, 'it's not safe. You'll have to wait.'

****

The minutes went by. Five. Six. Men surrounded the gap in the rubble. There were voices, shouts, and the men bent down, stretching their arms to lift something towards them. And suddenly, there she was. Her hair was filthy and her clothes covered in a dark dust. Two men held her as they crossed the rubble. Between them, she looked like a tiny bundle of rags and wet hair.

'Oh, hello boys,' said Mrs Winters, when she saw us. We rushed forwards, throwing our arms around her.

'Easy lads,' said the Chief Constable, his face serious.

'You're okay!' I said, trembling. 'I was so worried!'

'Yes,' she said, her voice suddenly breaking into a vicious cough. 'It's a good job that gargoyle kept the door to the stairs open, or it would have been the end of the line for me.'

'What happened?'

'A lucky escape,' she replied, smiling weakly. 'As the church was collapsing I ducked beneath the water and swam like mad. I reached the tower and managed to get in, but only just. I had to keep moving up the stairs as the water was rising. I must admit, it wasn't the happiest twelve hours of my life. But I'm still here. The trouble is, so is our furry friend.'

She burst into another round of furious coughing.

She was not well. Her face was as white as a sheet. I felt sad. Perhaps Mrs Winters was not as strong as I thought.

'What...what happened to the Lunar Rose?' she asked.

'I've got it,' I whispered. 'It's safe.' I'd put it at the bottom of my cupboard, beneath old toys I didn't play with any more.

'Keep it hidden,' she said weakly. 'It must not fall into the wrong hands. Now. I need...to...have a rest...' she said.

'We're going to get you to the hospital,' said the Chief Constable.

Mrs Winters tipped her head back and her eyes closed. Two men strapped her tiny body onto a stretcher and carried her towards an ambulance, its blue lights faintly flickering against the remains of St Cuthbert's.

Chapter Thirty-Three

An hour later, Mrs Winters was lying in a clean white bed in Rigor Mourtice hospital. Her body seemed frail within the sheets. On her cheek were three red stripes where the Werewolf had sliced her skin. The blood was crusted and an angry scab was forming on her skin.

I stood next to the bed and looked down. The Chief Constable stood behind me, at the door. After a moment she turned to look at me.

'Hello dear,' she said, her voice thin and soft.

I smiled at her. I wanted to say something but all the words left me.

'Have you found him?' she asked the Police.

'Our men are looking for the creature now,' said the Chief Constable.

Mrs Winters' eyes narrowed. 'I sincerely hope you know what you're dealing with.'

'I'm sure we can cope,' said the Chief Constable, but he hesitated before he spoke. A moment later, his mobile phone rang and he stepped out of the room to talk to the caller. I closed the door and returned to Mrs Winters.

She clutched my hand.

She tipped her head towards mine until our foreheads touched. She breathed out and I felt the warm air on the side of my face. She spoke in a low voice.

'James, you and Neville have shown remarkable courage. Whatever happens, don't let that bravery desert you. Be bold. All will be well in the end. Do you hear?'

'What about your infection?' I said. 'How will we deal with that?'

'Look in the manual,' she said. 'There's a section on antidotes. Everything you need is in there. I will help you if I can. Keep an eye on Clarence for me.'

'But I don't...' I said. Before I could finish, the door opened quietly and a nurse entered the room. It was time for Mrs Winters to get some rest, she said. I left the room, my head down. Without Mrs Winters I felt helpless. How would I do anything without her? How would I be able to get an antidote? The task before me felt huge.

In the corridor, an officer was now standing by the door to Mrs Winters' room, keeping guard. He looked down at me as I walked into the corridor. Twelve feet away, the Chief Constable was talking in a low voice to two other policemen. I listened carefully.

'...taken five miles downstream, Sir, in the town of Badly Duntoo. These pictures were taken at seven o'clock this morning. We're not sure when these tracks were fresh, but they could have been made at seven o'clock last night, after Rigor Mourtice was flooded. Our men are searching the area. So far, there is no sign of the...creature.'

The Chief Constable shook his head as his eyes flicked over several pieces of paper.

'Call HQ and alert them immediately,' he snapped. He looked up and saw me.

'James,' he said, holding out the photograph. 'Look at this. Can you confirm these are the markings of the creature?'

I looked at the picture. A black and white shot showed the

edge of the river, and the riverbank next to it. A couple of tree roots and plants were on the right hand edge of the picture. At the top, the edge of the water, seen from above. And in the photo's centre, a trail of large paw prints, going deep into the mud, then heading up the side of the riverbank.

'Yeah,' I said. 'That's him.'

****

The town was busy. Men in orange trousers strode around the town holding pipes that led to pumping machines, sucking up the mud and water. Cars were wiped clean, windows sprayed and doorsteps washed. The local shop sold out of buckets and mops. Heavy machinery climbed the hill to the reservoir to slowly rebuild its walls.

Reporters and photographers poured in from all over Noirshire. It didn't take them long to find me and Neville and ask us about our adventure.

The Noirshire Times ran a story, two days after the flood, with what Dad described as 'lurid headlines'. 'Our Teacher was a Monster!' said the paper in big black letters, and beneath it was a picture of Neville and me. The photographer told us to look 'a bit worried' for the picture, so Neville bit his lip and I had really wide eyes.

When I wasn't being bothered by journalists, I was followed by groups of kids from school who wanted my autograph. Our doorbell rang constantly. Mum and Dad got sick of kids knocking on the door. Neville was getting lots of visitors, too. He said we should start a fan club.

****

I pulled the key from its usual place under the flowerpot at the front door and twisted it in the lock. The door creaked a little as it swung open and we stepped inside.

'Funny,' said Neville. 'You can still smell the baking.'

'Yeah,' I smiled. 'It's not the same without her, though.'

I looked around at the pots of strange ingredients and the books on the shelf. Each day since the flood, I'd been to her house, usually with Dad watching suspiciously. The first time, I packed away all my things that were still there and put them in a box to take home. Then I went back each day to make sure Clarence had food and water. I'd checked the handbook was on the shelf, but I didn't mention it to Dad. He might have got suspicious and given it to the Police, or something.

'Somebody's pleased to see us,' said Neville, looking down at Clarence.

The cat twisted around my ankle, a purr vibrating in his neck. I put some food in Clarence's bowl. He miaowed loudly.

'I know you miss her,' I said. 'But don't worry. She'll be home soon, Clarence.'

****

'It's not been an easy time,' said Miss Lipps, her voice bellowing through the hall. 'And I know some of you are a little unsettled. But I think we should all thank James Small and Neville Heavy for their bravery in dealing with...erm...our tricky situation.'

As Miss Lipps continued talking, a spider landed on the floor of the hall. I scooped it up. I could feel the spider inside my palm. I showed Neville. He giggled into his hand. I let the beast drop onto Lucy's shoulder.

'These two boys,' said Miss Lipps, 'have shown amazing courage and bravery because...'

She was interrupted by a shrill scream. Lucy Black was pointing at the spider. I laughed. Neville sniggered. Miss Lipps rolled her eyes. I looked at Neville. He was giggling into his hand. 'Now who,' boomed Miss Lipps, 'did that?'

To be continued...

Suggestions for Teachers – Literacy Activities
based on 'Howl: A Small And Heavy Adventure'

1.   What do the children in your class think Grindell would eat for his tea? Ask them to write a fun and imaginative description.

2.   How does James feel when he arrives at Mrs Winters? Ask the children to write a diary entry describing James' experience during his first night in the house.

3.   Ask the children to imagine they are Grindell. What's it like? How do they feel? They can write a short story from Grindell's point of view, focusing on his secret. How does he hide it from the world?

4.   James and Neville go for a ride on Mrs Winters' moped. Describe their adventure. What do they see, hear and smell? Ask the children to try to capture the details in their descriptions.

5.   Try some Hallowe'en poems and stories. Focus on atmospheric descriptions of pumpkins in the dark etc. The spookier the better!